STAMPEDE

Three of them blow into the Wyoming town of Maverly that afternoon: Big Bill Spooner, José Murphy, and their leader Johnny Colt. Tired of being saddle tramps, they're looking to write off their debts and make a stake in the cattle business. So when Johnny pays a visit to a man who owes him money, and is instead made fifty-one-percent owner of a herd of nine hundred cattle, he and his pards agree to drive them to Deadwood and collect some cool thousands. But how far will they get through the worst stretch of Indian country in the West before they're scalped and their beef is stripped for jerky? When they join up with tougher-than-a-grizzly Clay Mixler's cattle drive for protection, they realize they've got more than Indians to worry about, including double-cross and bullets with their names on them . . .

STAMPEDE

DAN CUSHMAN

SAGEBRUSH
Large Print Westerns

First published in the United States by Fawcett

First Isis Edition
published 2019
by arrangement with
Golden West Literary Agency

A catalogue record for this book is available
from the British Library.

ISBN 978–1–78541–690–3 (pb)

PUBLISHED BY
F. A. THORPE (PUBLISHING)
ANSTEY, LEICESTERSHIRE

Set by Words & Graphics Ltd.
Anstey, Leicestershire
Printed and bound in Great Britain by
T. J. International Ltd., Padstow, Cornwall

This book is printed on acid-free paper

CHAPTER
ONE

There were three of them, and they had ridden a long way. On one side was Big Bill Spooner, slouched in the saddle as though to minimize his size; on the other was José Murphy, handsome, dark, and quick-eyed, with a guitar wrapped in the slicker behind his saddle; and in the middle was Jonathan Calhoun Colter, whom no one north of Texas knew by any name except Johnny Colt.

The road entered Maverly from the west, and their tired horses followed it without guiding, through scattering shacks of cottonwood logs, over a little rise, around the corrals of the De Luxe Livery Stable. There, with the dusty main street lying before them, Johnny Colt called a halt and sat at ease in the saddle, his hat slid back, its sweatband printed in a wet circle around his unruly brick-colored hair.

"There it is," he said. "Maverly. Queen city of the North Platte. I hope the hell it's worth the quart of dust we ate in getting here."

He had a slow Texas manner, a Southern drag in his speech, especially noticeable in his use of the word "here," which he broke into two syllables, "*hee-ah*."

1

José Murphy whispered, "Maverly," with his eyes almost closed. There was a smile at the tips of his white teeth. "Worth the treep? Worth one hundred treeps. Maverly, city of my dreams. Maverly weeth its gay señoritas, its pitfalls of pleasure!"

Big Bill Spooner, hearing him, jerked his big frame erect and took new interest in the town. He looked it all over, but it still wasn't much — thirty false-fronted buildings packed together as though, with all the public domain of Wyoming free for the taking, these few square feet were precious; and beyond, just the shacks, sheds, and rubbish heaps that were common to frontier towns everywhere.

A wrinkle formed between his eyebrows and he said in a voice unexpectedly high, "Gosh, Josie, it don't look like it was big enough to have many pitfalls."

"Well, what do you expect in a territory like Wyoming? You theenk you should have something beeg like Dodge City or New York? So maybe it is only a small town with seex pitfalls instead of twelve. Then we will visit them all twice and the girls will be twice as happy." He looked over at Johnny Colt. "Eh, Johnny, for ninety miles with nothing to drink except water you have told us of thees old friend who waited for you in Maverly — a friend with a potful of pesos only looking for a window to throw them out of. How is it now with his pesos? I tell you, that is one pot I would not mind having thrown at me."

"He's yonder," Johnny said placidly.

José, whose full name was José Julio Santiago Pérez García y Bolívar Murphy, let a laugh jerk his shoulders.

2

He gathered a ball of saliva from his dried mouth and spat. "So *he* is! He has blue eyes, perhaps? His name is maybe Genevieve?"

"To hell with you."

"He wears lace pants, thees man? And about the pesos — will you have more or fewer of them when you are through visiting him?"

"His name's Tom Mace, if you have to know. He's here hiding out because somebody would like to shoot the top of his head off. That's what was in the letter they delivered to me at Point of Rocks. I didn't tell you, Josie, because he doesn't want his hideout to be known, and you never developed the fine art of keeping your mouth shut."

"He is a fugitive!"

"Call it anything you want to."

"He is a coach robber?"

"He might be that, too. I never asked."

"And he said where his hideout was?"

"Yonder." With a cigarette just twisted into shape, Johnny Colt indicated a big, ornate, ramshackle hotel down the street. "I reckon that's it — the Hanover House."

"Blood of the dons! Here is truly a king among road agents, hiding not in some miserable cave in the badlands, but in a fine hotel."

Their horses had been drifting that way. José, admiring the hotel, lifted the Colt from the holster high on his waist. He did it with the air of one who enjoys the balance of a fine gun. "A magneeficent hotel!" His eyes were on a row of knobs that adorned a railing

3

around the veranda. "A wager, señor! Ten dollars on the first knob, no?"

"Put the gun away! We're causing no commotion here."

José laughed, and with a twist of his body aimed and fired. The bullet, sped with a young lifetime of practice, smashed one of the knobs and sent fragments of wood rattling across the veranda floor.

Johnny Colt cursed him, but there was a sudden pleasure in his blue eyes. He drew and fired in one deft movement, the bullet shattering the knob next to the shattered one.

"Tie score," he said. "Raise you ten."

José's horse, frightened by gunfire, fought around against the tight bridle and reared. When he came down, José was out of the saddle. He alighted with his boots set wide, holding the bridle with his left hand, the Colt in his right.

"No cheap bets, señor! It is here your José gets out of debt. Feefty dollars!" And without waiting for Johnny's answer, he fired again.

He broke a knob and Johnny Colt broke a knob. José, dragged by the pawing, bridle-fighting horse, saw his third shot go wide.

He got the animal quieted and tied to a hitch rack. Now miserable, he punched smoking cartridges from his gun, reloaded, and with a black book and stub pencil from his pocket he sat down on the edge of the plank walk to inscribe a figure.

"Where's my fifty?" Johnny asked him.

"Señor, I am bankrupt, without money, as you well know." He riffled the pages of the memorandum book, each filled with tiny notations. "Behold these debts. Has ever a man been bowed down under a load of debts like your poor José? Look, to you alone I owe the grand total of feefty thousand, four hundred and thirty dollars, and seex beets."

"I'll settle for that gunpowder roan bronc you left over at the T Bar M on Rock Creek."

"No! Listen while I tell you that to all my people is the debt a sacred obligation. Never do my people forget a debt. Behold while I swear that I will go on owing these moneys every last centavo to the last day of time!"

The eruption of gunfire had awakened Maverly from its afternoon stupor and brought men from doorways all along the street. A tall, hard-jawed man wearing a marshal's star came up and gave them a stern looking over.

"Evenin', seh," Johnny Colt said.

The marshal recognized the accent and said, "If you Texas boys have an idea that you're going to tear this town apart —"

"Marshal, this town of yours would be pretty small 'taters for men of our talents." The grin on Johnny Colt's face took all the fatigue and hardness away.

José cried, "Señor, you are looking at the three men who just took Denver apart, shingle for board, so that they are still looking for the roof of McQuade's Temple Bar. What would we be doing wasting our talent in such a miserable cow camp that it has only seex pitfalls of pleasure?"

A short, fat man with huge ears and jowels that hung down like a bullfrog's had come out on the hotel porch. He wore a diamond ring that made a hard twinkle in the sun.

"The owner?" Johnny asked, and without waiting for an answer said on the quiet to Big Bill Spooner, "You watch our Mex-Irish comrade and try to keep him out of trouble. I wasn't joking about the pesos. This is our chance to make a stake for ourselves. I mean a three or four-thousand-dollar stake, enough to set us up in the cattle business. I'm sick of being a saddle tramp, myself."

Bill said, "I want nothing to do with road agents, and if you —"

"Oh, that's just crazy talk. You ought to know you can't believe anything Josie says. Tom Mace never took a black dollar in his life. I don't know why he's hiding out, but I'll wager it has nothing to do with robbery."

He walked with his saddle-sprung cowboy manner across the street and up the steps to the porch. "Evenin', seh," he said to the fat man.

Florid and fighting his fury, the man cried in broken German, "You it vas dot shoot mine first-class hotel down? You know how much dot millwork cost me? Sixty cents a foot laid down in Cheyenne. *Ja*, sixty cents, and I had to have it freighted here yet. Why does everybody chop down mine place mit bullets when they want target practice? Listen while I tell you — cowboys do not deserve a first-class hotel mit sheets on bed. What cowboys deserve is a forkful of hay in back of the horses in a livery stable."

"If you don't mind, put mine in front of the horses."

"In *back* of the horses!"

"Well, seh, I'm sorry about the knobs." Johnny Colt looked so sincere that the German's temper came down a few degrees. "We thought that was what you had 'em up for. You see, seh, we noticed that some, of 'em had been shot off already."

He blew out his breath and said, "*Ja*. Pretty soon they will all be shot off, and then I suppose they will start in on mine cornices. You are maybe looking for a room?"

"It could be I am." The bartender from the hotel bar had come outside and was only a couple of steps away, listening. Johnny had seen him before, but he couldn't remember where. There was no reason to suspect him; it was just that he didn't want to mention the name of Tom Mace any more than necessary.

The German flung open the screen door, bowed, and said, "Then come in. Always in mine hostelry is a guest welcome, even if he shoots off mine knobs, which I will add to his bill."

The lobby was cool and deep shaded. It was hard to see while sun blindness put a flicker in his eyes. He followed the German, found the counter, and leaned against it. Slowly, things became visible. The German was across from him, flanked by potted palms. He dipped a pen in some sirupy-looking ink and offered it.

"Everyone must sign for room. Chust like in first-class Chicago hotel."

"Seh, I was always taught that the really *first-class* hotels were located in N'Orleans."

Johnny took the pen, but before signing, he let his eyes run down the register book, reading the names: J. G. Schrader, Louisville, Kentucky. Red Rathbone, Denver; The Bear Creek Kid; and on the bottom of the page, with a fine flourish and several ink blots, Ulysses S. Grant, White House, Washington, D.C.

"I see you have some distinguished guests."

"Oh, Grant, he iss not here." The proprietor laughed with a fat shake of his wattles. "The boys sometimes play chokes on me, but I don't care. Chust so they sign the book like in first-class hotel. Everything here first class."

Johnny leafed forward a page, still looking for Tom Mace's name, though he was sure it wouldn't be there. Mace, in his letter, had asked him to come quickly; he said that he was lying low at the Hanover House, looking for a chance to give some old friend a wagonload of silver dollars before a bunch of "low-yellow bushwackers put another bullet in me."

The ink had dried on the pen. He dipped it, and, working carefully, with the manner of one who did not write more than one hundred words a year, put down, "Johnny Colt, Texas."

The German had turned his back to look through the pigeonholes for a key. Johnny said in a soft voice, "You happen to have a guest here by the name of Tom Mace? I got a letter from him."

The German flinched. He turned, and as he did so his eyes darted to the front of the room and back again.

"Tom Mace?" He spoke in a wheezy voice. He seemed to have a hard time getting his breath. Then he

8

recovered himself and put an expression of rage on his face. He doubled both fists, lifted them overhead, and drove them to the desk in unison. "You ask about Tom Mace? That cheat? That whisky-drinking drunk? You ask about him, I ask who is going to pay the three days' room rent he left me mitout."

Mace had never run out on a chippy debt like that in his life, and Johnny Colt knew it. The German was talking for somebody's benefit. He turned with a casual slouch of his body, one elbow on the counter, and saw that a man was seated by the front window partly hidden by a tattered copy of the Cheyenne Weekly Sun.

Johnny's eyes passed over him as over any stranger. He seemed more interested in his cigarette, dragged, and said, "Tom's up to his old tricks. He owes every innkeeper between here and Sonora."

Above the newspaper he could see the upper half of the man's face. He was about thirty years old. His eyes were small, his cheekbones high with patches of freckles over them. He was medium in height, dehydrated by outdoor living. His boots had recently been shined. He wore gray serge trousers rather than the usual Levis; they were large for his legs, blousing over where his guns were tied down on each thigh. *Two guns.* You heard of two-gun men all the time, but it wasn't often you caught sight of one in the flesh. It was only natural that Johnny Colt should look at him longer on that account.

Johnny had his right hand in his pocket. He found the letter. It was compressed into a small, closely folded square. He took it out, closed in his fist, and, moving so

9

the German was hidden from the gunman's eyes, laid it on the counter.

The German stared down at the letter, a lump of rough paper, dirty and worn from long carrying. He reached, took it. His fingers had the jumps and he almost dropped it. Johnny Colt filled the time by talking in his easy drawl:

"Yeah, that's Tom Mace. Worst petty thief between heah and the Pecos. Is for a fact. I found that out the hard way. He still owes me eighty-five in trail-drivin' money since a year ago August, and anybody that'll beat a man out of that kind of dirt-and-sweat wages is next lowest thing to a carpetbagger. I'd hoped to catch up with him heah and collect."

The German read the few scrawled lines of the letter, refolded it, and slid it back, doing it all without moving his shoulders. Still not changing position, he reached beneath the counter and got out a key tied to a big wooden tag. Holding it carefully so the key would not jingle, he slipped it inside Johnny Colt's shirt. His face had been florid, then yellowish pale, and now florid again. Sweat glistened on his broad cheeks. He took a very deep breath and puffed his cheeks in blowing it out.

Johnny said, "What was Tom doing here, anyhow? Last I heard he was running a little haywire spread down by Bear Creek, fattening the fallen beef he bought at ten cents a hundred off the trail herds."

"He vas — mit trail herd." He got the words out. He took another deep breath. He was afraid of the gunman, so afraid he was sick. Johnny knew how it was.

He had felt like that himself. It was no disgrace to be scared. It was what a man did in spite of being scared that counted.

Johnny said, "Trail boss got sick of him, I suppose, and ran him out."

"*Ja*." The German sounded more confident. He was over the worst of it now. "He haff — some trouble. He got shot. *Ja*. Wounded. Some drunken brawl, maybe. Ach, he vas no goot. Mine medicines he used. Mine bed he slept in. Mine whisky he drank. Always something more he wanted. 'Put this on bill, put that on bill, you are such a fine fellow.' Then one day, pfft! He is gone and I am holding bag filled mit nothings."

"Think he went to Cheyenne?"

"Perhaps. Or Denver."

"Nobody saw him leave?"

"He has friend mit freight outfit. Hodges. I think in hooligan wagon he hid out and rode to Cheyenne."

"Why, then, maybe I'll drift that way."

The gunman was still hidden by the paper. He had not moved all the while, not even allowing the page to rustle. He had hung on every word. Now, as Johnny started away, he let the paper fall, yawned, stretched, and spat on the floor. He was taking his good, long look.

The German said, "Find him for me and I will giff you half of all you collect."

"All I want is my eighty-five dollars," Johnny said, and walked through the archway to the bar.

The room was empty, and momentarily he was beyond the gunman's view. He took the key from his shirt. The number 26 was burned in the tag. He slipped it inside his pants pocket. Twenty-six. That would probably be on the second floor. He surmised that there'd be a rear stairway. Anyhow, there was no hurry. He would wait until dark. That gunman out there was suspicious already.

The bartender came in, served Johnny a bottle of St. Louis beer, took a small pony glass for himself, and said, "I seen you before. Knew when you rode into town, and I been trying to place you ever since. Now I remember. It was down in Corbus."

"Johnny Colt," he said, and they shook hands.

"Sure, Johnny Colt. I tended bar there in Corbus City all through the cattle war. I was there the day you shot it out with Nelson Spangelo in the middle of Main Street. I was there the day the militia showed up, too." He was grinning. "Saw 'em take you and the Spaniard and about fifteen more down to Fort Ludloe. What ever happened down there, anyhow?"

Johnny Colt drank the beer. It was very cold from the ice tub. He looked at the bartender and through him. He waited until he was all through with the bottle before answering:

"I forgot. I dug a deep hole, and scraped all that ruckus inside it." The back-bar mirror told him that the gunman had changed position and was watching him. "Who is he?" he asked, tilting his head.

The bartender seemed surprised that he didn't know. "Why, that's Ed Ward."

"Live here in Maverly?"

"He's been here before."

"How long this time?"

"Why, he hit town three or four days ago."

"All alone?"

"There's a fellow with him."

"What's his name?"

The bartender suddenly became reticent. "I don't know. I don't ask about names. I just do my job."

He knew, all right, but he didn't want to be dragged into any of Johnny Colt's trouble.

Johnny grinned and said, "I don't blame you. I don't blame you a damned bit."

CHAPTER
TWO

Johnny Colt drifted outside and down the street. He looked for José Murphy and Big Bill Spooner without seeing them or expecting to see them. José would be exploring the pitfalls and Big Bill would be trying to keep him out of trouble. He ate at Hong Gim's San Francisco Beanery, and played out a stack of whites in the faro game at the Green Front.

It seemed like a long wait. Ed Ward, with the tied-down guns giving him an awkward look, came in, pretended not to see him, and wandered on. As evening settled the town filled up a little, but it was always quiet at that time of year. Towns like Maverly were all alike — they lay half dormant through ten months waiting for the golden harvest of the beef roundup.

The darkness finally suited him, so he cashed in and walked out the back door.

He stopped in the shadow of some sheds to see if anyone would follow him. Nobody did. Walking casually, he circled back to the Hanover House and waited again. There were some outside stairs, as he'd supposed. He climbed them, groped his way down a dark hall, lighted a match.

Number 26. A lamp was burning inside. Its light came in a thin slit beneath the door. He listened, heard the slight complaint as somebody moved.

The match burned his fingers. He cursed, flipped it away. The man inside was sitting very still now, listening.

"Tom!" he said with his lips close against the panel. "Tom, is that you in there?"

The light went out, then a husky voice said, "Who is it?"

"Johnny. Johnny Colt."

"Oh." He still sounded suspicious. "Have you got a key?"

"Yes."

"Well, open the door. Open it, but don't come in. Just stand for a second so I can see you."

Johnny knew what was on his mind. He thought Ed Ward might have marched him there at the point of a gun. He fitted the key, turned it in the lock, and let the door swing open. He could see where the window was, but vaguely, for the shade had been pulled. The remainder of the room was a mere shadow outline. The air was filled with the camphor odor of liniment.

Tom laughed with a gruff relaxation of tension and said, "Well, come on in, you wuthless saddle tramp, and light the lamp."

The lamp revealed him, an undersized, grizzled man with very bright blue eyes, propped up in bed with a .45-caliber Colt between his knees. He had a big chaw of tobacco in one cheek, and while looking at Johnny he leaned over to aim at a small china spittoon. He made a direct hit.

"Who you expect?" Johnny asked. "Maybe Ed Ward?"

"Him or Kiowa Jim."

"Kiowa! I heard he got killed at Redpath two years ago."

"That's what should have happened. They should have hung him, but they didn't. They held him for the next term of co't and he busted out of jail."

Tom looked thinner than he remembered, and a pallor mottled his brown skin. He'd lost some blood and it had left him weak.

Johnny said, "Shot and hiding out in this room — what in hell's going on?"

"I ain't bad off here. First rest I've had since I got tossed in that Yankee prison durin' the wah."

"If it's just Ed Ward and Kiowa —"

"If it was, I'd shoot em, and maybe I will before I'm through. No, I didn't send for you because of them. I got bigger pork than that on the fire. It's just that I'm hipshot and bedrid, and that I need a job done. Me, I'll git along. That's a good Dutchman down there. He packs me grub and keeps the visitors away. I sent for you because I needed you for something else. You open that bureau drawer. You'll find a couple of articles there, one for you and one for me."

The bureau contained a folded legal document and a pint of Old Haversill's bourbon.

Johnny held them out. "Take your choice."

"I'm no idiot. I'll take the likker."

Tom Mace had a big one out of the pint and tucked the remainder away beneath his blanket. "Sorry, but I'm not treating you out of this. That damn Dutchman has me on rations, pint in the morning and pint at night. He's afraid I'll see animals. By cripes, a man sees enough animals crawling around this hotel whether he drinks whisky or not. Go ahead and read that document."

Johnny held it to the light. The paper, sealed by a notary, signified that Mr. Jonathan Colter, better known under the name of Johnny Colt, was hereunder certified to be 51-per-cent owner of nine hundred longhorn cattle, bearing the Rocking A brand, territorial registry of Colorado, at that inst. somewhere on the trail in Wyoming Territory.

"What does it mean?"

"Means what it says. Those are the critters I gathered down south in Coloraydo and hand-fed until they put me in the cattle business. Range got poor, and them Yankee buyers wouldn't pay me as much as seven dollars a head, so I trail-herded nawth. Now I'm hipshot, I not able to trail-herd nothing. If you want four-fifty head of longhorns, all you need do is catch up with 'em and make your claim. Say, you didn't think I sure enough did have a wagonload of silver dollars on account of that letter!"

"Where is your herd?"

"Maybe just over the Nawth Platte. Hell, how do I know where they are, me flat on my back and them gunmen waitin' for me?"

"Tom, you're just being hopeful. Sitting Bull's taken over that country, from Platte almost to Yellowstone. If you left nine hundred head of cattle up there, I'll wager they're just so much squaw jerky by this time."

"I wasn't alone. I thought you knew. I joined up with Mixler. He's got the biggest damn herd of cattle ever went through Wyoming. Him and half a dozen other ranchers. My stock wasn't more'n a tenth part of it. You take that paper along. You show it to Mixler. He's tougher'n a grizzly, but he'll honor it."

Johnny thrust the paper in his pocket. "Sure, I'll take charge of your cattle, but a half interest is too much."

"A half is too little. Now keep quiet and listen to what all I got to say, and you'll agree with me. I threw in with Mixler's outfit because it was a big one and I figured he could fight his way through the Injuns. However, Mix is driving straight nawth across the Yellowstone to a place called Deergrass Valley. But you and our steers go only halfway. You and our steers will turn off at the Belle Fourche and cross the divide to Sundance Creek, and then —"

"Then *that's* where those Sioux squaws begin making jerky."

"Why, they might, and again they might not. It all depends on a number of things. Sitting Bull will have his scouts on the herd, I suppose, but if you make the break quick enough, take 'em by surprise, and drive all night, you'll get 'em to Deadwood before they'll get force enough to attack. Go like I say, over that Sundance divide, and you can run 'em mighty near all the way. By grab, for a long haul, you give me a lean old

18

line-back steer, he'll outlast a horse. I don't care how you do it, Johnny, but *get 'em to Deadwood*. Those miners have been living on beans and jack rabbit ever since Sitting Bull left the agency and cut off the freight roads. Know what a nine-dollar steer would be worth in that camp?"

"Twenty?"

"Ha, twenty! Why, in Deadwood they toss twenty-dollar nuggets to the Chinee. *A hundred.*" He rose in bed as though he expected Johnny to contradict him. "Yes, that's what I said! A hundred dollars! And they'll take the whole herd at that price. There are twelve thousand miners in the Black Hills, Army estimate, and nine hundred steers aren't going to go too damned far."

"Split with you, forty-sixty."

"No, its half and half. That's a he-man split." Talking had left him a trifle tired. He had another from the bottle. "Did I tell you about that Dutchman having me down to a quart a day?"

Mixler, Johnny was thinking. That would be Mixler of the Leon, down in Texas. The Leon was east of Johnny's part of Texas, but Mixler was the sort of fellow who got to be known far and wide. He could even remember the brand. It was a Bar M, made in the manner generally referred to as M on a Rail.

"Mixler. Clay Mixler. What's a big old outfit like that doing on the trail?"

"He's quitting Texas. Texas ain't what she used to be, Johnny. It's even worse than when you left. The war bled her, and the carpetbaggers strangled her, and now the drought is finishing her. The big outfits are through down there. You know who else is on the move to new grass? The Haltmans. Yes, the Haltmans! They were so busted that Mixler had to stake 'em to get 'em out of the country, and here old Saltis Haltman had so damned much money he bought that seat in Congress."

Johnny was seated, his chair tilted against the wall. It was an old story, the fate of Texas, but he heard Tom out, then he said, "Now tell me the rest of it. Why'd they try to kill you?"

"It's got nothing to do with the herd. You get them through to Deadwood. That'll be a full-time job without adding my ruckus to it. I got a bone-chipped hip or something, but that's not important. I'll be around, all right. I'll take care of —"

"Mixler try to get you?"

"He's mean, I'll admit, but he wouldn't bushwhack a man. If Mix decided to get you, he'd walk right up on. those stud-horse legs of his and break your neck. I know how folks felt about Mix, but don't go up there with a chip on your shoulder. Mix is —"

"The Haltmans?"

"Hell, Johnny, they're all right. They ain't high and mighty like they used to be down yonder. You'd hardly know the Haltman boys."

"Why'd Kiowa and that gunman follow you here?"

"Well, if you got to know, it was like this: Mixler was looking for men to get that herd through Injun country, and it wasn't easy. He took what men he could find. Some of 'em were on the loose and went for the hell of it, and some joined up because they had the law on their tails. I knew that, and I should have kept my mouth shut, but I didn't."

"And they laid for you."

"Row over a monte game. Lobo named Andy Rasmussen. Called him plenty. Told him I knew he was wanted for a Missouri Pacific mail-car robbery they pulled back in '72. Guess he and some of the boys thought I intended to turn 'em over to Army law when we got up to Fort Keogh. So they decided I was a good man to put out of the way. They got me with a bushwack bullet one night, and it wasn't so much, but I knew I wouldn't stand any more chance than likker at a Blackfoot camp meeting if I stayed with the herd. I lit out, Johnny."

"How long you aim to live in this bed?"

"It's not bad. I'm getting a good rest."

"How long have those gunmen been waiting?"

"Since the day after I came. I hid out in this room, hoping they'd go. They didn't. They stuck tight. I'll lay gold agin' greenbacks that Ed Ward is right down in the lobby this minute. Johnny, you look at me. You think I'm yellow?"

"If I said yes, you'd shoot me dead."

"Johnny, I been kicking around the country for a heap of years, no roof over my head, no grub but pan bread and jerky, never so much as one gold piece to rub against another, and now I see the chance, I want to make my stake. You take those steers through for me, Johnny. You and Big Bill and the Mex. By grab, if there's anybody that can take 'em through, you can. The Mex *is* with you, ain't he?"

"He's along."

"You put him out on the point. No Sioux will harm him. They think crazy men are the chosen of God."

CHAPTER
THREE

When he left Tom's room the last luminous light of evening was gone from the sky. No moon yet. He had to grope his way through the alley to the street.

The marshal saw him and walked across to meet him. "I been told you're Johnny Colt."

"They call me that."

"We don't back up very easy from a man's reputation in this town."

With his hat back from his unruly hair and a grin on his face, it was hard to imagine Johnny Colt having carved out a reputation anywhere. He didn't even carry his Colt gun-fighter style. He said, "Oh, the knobs! I already discussed them with the German, but if it makes you feel better, you pick up the pieces and I'll have Big Bill Spooner glue 'em back on. I will for a fact, just as soon as we get back from Deadwood."

"I don't give a damn about the target practice. What I'm talking about is that ornery Mexican pal of yours. He's looking for trouble."

"Again? Never saw anything as crazy as a Mex-Irish half-breed. Inherits the worst traits of both races. Throw a knife with one hand and a brick with the other. Cries in his beer and fights duels. Eats Mulligan stew and washes it down with red wine. You'll never believe, seh, what I've gone through for that man. I reckon I'd have let 'em hang him that time down in Mascalero, only he owed me the sum of forty-one thousand dollars, and I couldn't afford it. Who's he having the ruckus with?"

"He's making love to Terry Slavin's wife. *Terry Slavin!*"

"Slavin, Slavin," Johnny repeated, as though trying to remember, although Slavin, a dance-hall operator, had a gunman's reputation that reached from Dodge to the Yellowstone.

He said, "Why, I wouldn't want anything to happen to one of your taxpayers. Where is all this going on?"

"At Slavin's — the Dublin Bar."

They walked together down platform sidewalks. The Dublin was a rambling, flimsy place, a boxlike two stories, unpainted, and though only a couple of years old, already warped out of shape. As they neared, the rapid twang of a guitar and the musical lilt of José's voice came to them. He was singing in Spanish — one of those hundred-stanza border songs.

Johnny Colt found himself walking in time. He wanted to close his eyes and hum the tune. He'd heard it a thousand times, but never like José did it. That Mex-Irish could really sing. He could sing like no one else Johnny Colt had ever heard.

"*Por mi amiga señorita,*" the voice sang with a perfect, lyric flexibility through the cool night air, "*la vida y el corazón.*"

How the hell, Johnny was thinking, could a man with a voice like that do the things José had done? It was enough to make you lose faith in the human race.

"You hear that?" the Marshal cried. "You hear that song he's singing?"

"Good, isn't it?"

"That's a Mex love song. Do you think Slavin's going to stand around and let a greaser make love to his wife?"

There was a slight hardening of Johnny's voice as he said, "It might just make a difference which greaser it is."

"If you think Slavin's the type that gets scared out by a cheap rep —"

"Well, I say good for Slavin."

Almost everyone in Maverly seemed to be jammed inside the Dublin — a combination saloon, hotel, and music hall of the type commonly referred to as a shebang, but they were quiet, listening to the song. The press of men stopped them, and Johnny had to stand tall to see José, who was at the back of the room, one boot on a chair, deft fingers finding the strings of the guitar, his eyes on the face of a thin-featured woman in scanty spangles who was taking her ease, roosting on the edge of an unused poker table. She was pretty, but Johnny had seen prettier.

"Where's Mrs. Slavin?" he asked.

"Why, right there on the card table. He's singing the song to her, like I said."

"Well, I'll be damned!" Johnny jerked back his head and laughed. "She took off her Mother Hubbard dress someplace along the line, didn't she?"

"What do you mean by that?"

"I mean Slavin shouldn't put his wife in a bird cage like this, undressed like that, unless he expects her to be treated like one of the girls. You know, I have a hunch she *is* one of the girls."

"This is Slavin's place. He'll do as he likes. Now, you listen — he'll kill the Mex for that. I don't want any killings in this town. I been hired to stop it. You rebs are always complaining about the deal you get in these Northern cattle camps, then when a man tries to help you —"

"Us rebs can take care of ourselves."

He turned away and walked to the bar. Big Bill Spooner saw him and came lunging through the crowd. He was out of breath and sweating. Worry showed on his broad face.

"Kid, he's headed for trouble. You know whose woman he's after this time? Slavin's!"

"Well, that's what comes from living where there's a shortage of women. What are you drinking?"

"I'm not drinking anything. Johnny, you listen here. You know who Slavin is? He's bad medicine. He can shoot out the eye of a snake at ten paces. He —"

"Can he name which eye, like Josie?"

"This is nothing to joke about. Josie's in no shape to fight. Look at him back there. You ought to see the likker he's taken on. If Slavin comes in here, he'll have his boys with him, and they'll shoot him dead."

26

Johnny felt sorry for Big Bill. He'd seen the fellow go through a place like this and turn it into a shambles, but he was sentimental, especially with José, and at that moment he was almost in tears. Johnny felt a special way about Big Bill. Probably he felt toward Bill like Bill felt toward José Murphy.

"Johnny, we got to get him out of here. He ain't got good sense like we have."

"Your old man owns half the cows in California. If *you'd* had good sense you wouldn't be here, saddle-tramping from one burned-out range to the other, wondering where your next grub pile will come from. You'd be home with your feet under his table. So let's not talk about having better sense than Josie. Only criticism I have of Josie's good sense is the looks of that woman he picked. I think I could find better. Even in Maverly. Now, wipe your nose and have a drink."

José was singing:

> "Ay, ay, ay, ay!
> Canta y no llores!"

The rhythm increased. The woman, caught by its spirit, sprang atop the table and started to swing her scantily clad body in a willing but misguided imitation of a fandango.

José played twice through the piece, leading her to a spirited climax. He finished with a loud whang of the guitar and cried, "Señorita, I have seen the fandango in Ciudad Chihuahua, I have seen it in Monterey, but never have I seen the fandango danced as I have seen it

27

thees night. You are the spirit of wine, you are the gazelle of the prairie. Stand on the table while I kiss your tiny slippered toe. I will kiss your ankle! I will kiss your knee. I will kiss —"

A man had hurled his way through the crowd. He shouted, "Keep your black hands off'n her, you dirty greaser!"

It was Slavin. Johnny Colt had met him in Denver a couple of years before, but he'd have known anyway. He was heavy and florid. A hard hat roosted on the back of his head. He wore a pearl-gray vest with embroidered horseshoes and jockey's caps. Across the front of the vest hung a gold chain set with natural nuggets. His coat was open, revealing the pearl butts of two long-barreled Smith and Wesson .44's.

José lovingly laid down the guitar. He used only his left hand. Then he scrutinized the man and said, "Eh? You were talking to me in those words? And who are you, señor?"

"I'm Slavin, and I don't bother to mar up my gun butts by cutting notches for Mexicans."

Flattered and wishing to hold the center of the stage, Mrs. Slavin screamed, held her head like an actress about to faint, and walked partly between them as she got down off the table.

Slavin shouted, "Get away from him, Queenie. I don't want you getting blood on your new dress."

She cried out again and twisted out of the way. Slavin had taken half a step. He was hunched forward. His big hands dangled from long arms from sloping shoulders. José seemed to be in no position to draw. He

28

carried his gun high, at the middle of his abdomen, the butt toward the right, gambler style. It seemed to be a long way from his hand, and not right to be grabbed in a hurry, anyway.

Slavin cried, "Get out of my place!"

"Go to the devil, señor!"

Slavin suddenly straightened, with both hands coming up, weighted by the heavy .44's. José, looking casual, swung around, and the Colt was there, aimed across his body. Slavin had been hopelessly outdrawn.

"A wager, Señor Johnny!" José cried. The Colt exploded across his words. The bullet, aimed low, tore along the floor, left Slavin's right boot in shreds. Johnny Colt, drawing with an automatic hitch of his body a quarter second later, blasted the heel of Slavin's other boot.

The twin bullet shocks, coming from crossed directions, knocked the saloonkeeper's feet from under him. He was down. One of the guns had fallen, the other was pinned under his hip. He tried to jerk the gun free without realizing that his own weight was holding it.

Men stampeded. A bartender came up with a sawed-off shotgun. He tried to get around the end of the bar, but the sudden rush of men carried him to the wall. Others, also employees of Slavin's, were caught among the card tables.

Big Bill shouted, "Let's get to hell out of here!"

He seized José by the arm and dragged him along.

"My guitar!" José wailed.

"I got it."

Johnny Colt followed with his gun still drawn. He hesitated at the door. The bartender had got free with his shotgun and had leaped atop a keg by the wall. Johnny aimed a .45 slug that tore splinters by his cheek and sent him in a sprawling dive for cover.

Bill pulled José past him through the door. José, struggling but helpless beneath the big fellow's strength, was saying, "Your solicitude is very touching, *amigo*, but I do not intend to retire from the field and leave that beautiful young girl for such a swine. Weeth your chivalry you would be a peon in Chihuahua."

"I ain't going to let you get killed. Not with all that money owing me, I'm not."

They were outside, and it seemed very dark. A cellar had been dug back of the Dublin, but no building had been constructed over it, and now it had become the receptacle for ashes and empty bottles. After groping they located a catwalk on prop poles that ran along the rear of the building. They cut around a Chinese laundry and reached the street.

Men ran past them, drawn by the sounds of excitement at the Dublin.

"You are pulling my arm out by the roots," José kept saying.

"I'm saving your worthless hide."

"Where are we going?"

"I don't know." Bill looked at Johnny Colt. "Where are we going?"

"Deadwood."

José said, "Deadwood! Are you loco? Deadwood is six sleeps to the north through five thousand warlike

Sioux all weeth repeating guns. Why would we go to Deadwood when here is Maverly and I have visited only two pitfalls? You theenk perhaps I am saving my hide from that Irishman? I am Irish, too, the half part of me, and that half cries out —"

"Stop it, Josie. If it was just Slavin, I'd say go back and to hell with you. But something else has come up. I'm talking about that wagonload of pesos. I just saw Mace. It's on the level. He's giving us a chance to make a stake for ourselves."

José went along a little more easily, then, though he still kept looking back at the Dublin.

Big Bill said, "You mean there *is* a wagonload of money?"

"Well, that was just a figure o' speech. What he was really talking about were some longhorns he wants put into Deadwood if we can do it without leaving our hair on Sitting Bull's medicine stick."

"There'd be a stake in that for us?"

"A stake so big that even Josie could pay his debts."

José laughed and said, "Ha! Now you are joking! There is not in all Wyoming Territory enough pesos to pay the debts of José Julio Santiago Pérez García y Bolívar Murphy. For my debts have I fled Coahuila and Chihuahua both. For my debts have both my father's and my mother's families disinherited me. Has ever a man been burdened by debt like your poor José?"

The upper end of Main Street was almost deserted. They crossed to the W Bar M wagon freight yards, toward a feed stable where Big Bill had left the horses.

Johnny said, "Funny I didn't see anything of Ed Ward or Kiowa Jim down at the Dublin."

"Kiowa! That half-breed killer? He is in town?"

"He's here, gunning for Tom Mace."

"But why —"

"I'll explain all I know about it when we get out on the trail."

Johnny kept thinking about Ed Ward and Kiowa. It would be natural for them to be down at the Dublin like everyone else, but he hadn't seen them. He looked back at the big black silhouette of the Hanover House.

A sudden fear for Tom Mace made him hesitate. Then he told himself that he wouldn't have to worry about old Tom. Not while he stayed there with that .45 between his knees. He'd rather pull a badger out of a barrel than Tom out of that room.

José said, "There is much of thees I do not understand."

"There's a whole hell of a lot I don't understand, either."

The freight yard was a couple of acres in extent, surrounded on two sides by sheds, on the other two by a fence of split cottonwood rails. In the middle, rising in a high silhouette against the night sky, was a windmill tower and a water tank. The wind that flowed across Wyoming day and night made the windmill turn with a steady creak, working a pump rod. Water had filled the tank. It overflowed with a musical trickle. Here, a hundred yards from Main Street, the silence of the prairie night already asserted itself and they began to notice such slight sounds.

There'd been movement somewhere. It put Johnny Colt on his guard. He hadn't expected trouble until that moment. He thought he'd left danger behind at the Dublin.

"This way," he said, "around the water tank. I'd stay clear of that shed."

Bill said, "Johnny, we put the horses —"

"Come along."

"What the —"

He was watching the warehouse, the platform, the black space beneath the platform. From the shadow of a shed he saw a glimmer on blued steel. He reacted instantly. He rammed Big Bill in one direction and José in the other, and dove forward to the wagon-rutted earth, drawing his gun as he fell.

Gunfire from two points tore the night with flame and concussion. He felt the wind roar of lead passing over him. He checked the impulse to fire back. His own movement, the strange surroundings, the dark, and the divergent points of flame momentarily baffled him. He rolled over on the earth, came to one knee as the guns blasted a second time. They were fifty or sixty yards off.

"Keep going!" he hissed at José and Big Bill, who were at his left, behind him.

He was no longer baffled. He concentrated on the closer of the guns, fired as fast as his thumb could hook the hammer, fired on the move, from one knee, from a standing position, from one knee again.

He kept going in a weaving, running crouch. He could hear the guns of Big Bill and José. He reached the partial protection of cribwork timbers supporting the water tank.

The shooting suddenly stopped. He got his breath. Water dripped on him. His gun was empty. On one knee he punched hot cases from the magazine and reloaded.

He'd left gunsmoke behind; now it caught up with him on the wind, a sulphury odor. He tried to listen. The close creak of the pump killed off any slighter sounds of movement, though he could hear doors slamming a hundred yards off along Main Street, the shouting voices of men wondering what the new batch of shooting could be.

Nobody was coming to investigate. Nobody would. Not even that big, rough marshal who'd been hired to stop such things.

Big Bill and José were yonder, crouched in the shadow behind a rubbish heap of barrels and packing cases. He couldn't help laughing. What a hell of a spot! A bullet would fly through the whole flimsy mass.

He got to his feet. Gun ready, he walked around the tank cribbing, around the watering trough.

The moon had been hidden by clouds. It was ready to reappear. Its light would pin him down in the middle of that barren freight yard.

He sprinted for the loading platform and was almost there before guns started to pound.

He made the last yards at a long, striding leap, let his legs buckle, and rolled to a stop beneath the platform.

Both the platform and the freight house beyond were supported by piles about three feet high. They gave concealment, and yet he could move as he pleased.

34

He crawled a distance, and fired, and crawled again. He cupped his hands and shouted across the yard:

"Bill! I'll keep 'em busy from here. You get yourself and Josie out of that rat's nest."

He kept creeping from post to post, firing, drawing a shot, answering it. The bushwhackers had lost their enthusiasm. They kept giving ground. The floor, close overhead, held in the sound, and every gunshot deafened him.

He'd fired the gun dry. He reloaded from the loops of his belt, and shot it dry again. The barrel was hot. Powder fouling had made the mechanism hard to operate. Each cartridge case stuck, and he set his teeth and cursed when, he had to punch it out. Sometime he'd invent a grease to put on cartridge cases that wouldn't wear off or burn off so a man's gun wouldn't go sour on him after the first dozen and a half shots. Denver papers told about a Belgian that had invented a powder that didn't smoke at all. That'd be the solution — either that or stay out of trouble.

He kept weaving through the piles, pawing spider webs from his face, and reached the rear fence.

"Bill?"

He hadn't seen him. It surprised him when the big fellow's voice came from only a few steps off.

"Yeah."

"Josie with you?"

"That damn greaser! You know, what he did? Went back for his guitar! I shouldn't have let him. I should have knocked him over the head and drug him, whether he liked it or not."

"Quit worrying about Josie. He'll live to be eighty and die of rheumatism."

They waited in the shadow of the rear fence. Once again the creaking windmill was the loudest sound in the night.

"Bill! Where are you, Bill?" It was José, coming across the yard.

"Here, and don't show yourself."

"Ha! They could hit nothing." He was rubbing dirt off the guitar. He kissed it and talked to it. "My sweetheart. Did you theenk your José would go away and leave you? Johnny, what is happening to thees country? It is going to the dogs that they would shoot a man for playing the guitar and making love."

Johnny said, "I don't want to hurt your pride, but *this* bushwhack wasn't Slavin's doing. They weren't after you. They were after me."

"But why?"

"For the same reason they tried to gun down old Tom Mace. And I'll wager it has nothing to do with any Missouri Pacific mail-car robbery, the way Tom tried to tell me. More like there's somebody else would like the job of delivering nine hundred head of longhorn beef to the minin' city of Deadwood."

They saddled and hunted back streets through town until the broad northern sweep of moonlit prairie lay ahead of them.

"Just the same," said José after a long silence, "those bullets came very close to my guitar."

CHAPTER
FOUR

They made a dry camp and slept under the stars. At dawn they saw Maverly on the flats behind them, perfect in miniature, apparently only a long gunshot away through the clear, rarefied atmosphere. They rode on at an easy pace to the willow-choked bottoms of the Little Muddy, where they made a fire for coffee and baked a pan of doughgod bread.

At noon Maverly was still visible, but not with the old pin-point sharpness. Heat waves spoiled it, took away the rectangular lines of the buildings, smeared their reflections. It looked like something painted on the flat prairie, shimmering, threatening to rise like a mirage on the hot air.

José balled some saliva off his tongue, spat, and wiped his lips on the back of his hand. "Miserable town of only seex pitfalls! Deadwood, now thees is a town of which men sing. Johnny, do you know what I will do when I get to Deadwood? First I will buy new clothes from one end to the other. Then in a barber chair I will have a shave all over my face except for my lip, where I will leave a mustache. Then weeth tonic on my hair —"

"When I get to Deadwood I'm going to have a piece of dried apple pie that big," Big Bill said in his treble.

"Sometimes I lay awake at night and think about apple pie. And pickles. I'd give ten dollars, cash money, for just one pickle."

José said, "Johnny, what is your ruling passion? Food for Big Bill, wine and women for me. Tell me, what made you a bum, drifting from range to range, weeth-out a pot to make coffee in or a window to throw it out of and no good to yourself or anybody?"

Johnny started to laugh it off, then he pulled his horse around suddenly and said, "You want to know why I left Texas? I'll tell you. It was on account of a woman. Pretty and young with yellow hair and dark eyes. Ever see that combination?"

"In woman I have seen all combinations. But tell me more about her."

"And shape? She was like this, and this, and in between she had a waist so slim you could put your two hands around it. She was a *gal*, Josie. And she was the real reason I left Texas."

José was breathless. "She married another and broke your heart!"

"She was real quality. Big-mansion quality. Born to wear silk and sleep in a bed with a canopy over it, but just the same she'd have followed me right up the trail — log shanty, dishpan, dirt floor. She was my woman, if I'd said the word. But I didn't. I rode off and I never saw her again."

"Her father chase you off weeth a gun."

"No, Josie. I just rode off. Tell you why I did it. I'd been seeing her one night, and I started back to Daddy Barlow's, where I'd been helping while his foreman was in San Antonio being doctored. Rode through the Mex end of town. Didn't go that way because it was shorter. Point is, I rode that way because of a little cantina there and a girl they called La Favorita. She used to do the fandango with her skirts pulled up to here. She liked me, too. Me and twenty others, depending on who had the most wine money in his pocket. I knew that, and knew I had the sweetest little girl in the world waiting for me at the other end of town, but still I didn't have the strength inside me to ride on home. Facts of life. You see, it'd be that way always. I just didn't have the moral fiber to be a married man."

José smiled with a flash of his extremely white teeth and whispered, "Keed, tell me about thees Favorita girl."

"Y'know, there's something funny. I ran onto her again years afterward over in Casa Miguel. I wouldn't have recognized her, but she knew me. She'd married a Mex corral keeper and was carrying a basket of wash on her head."

"I'll wager she was thees fat and had seex kids already. How many looked like you?"

"Oh, go to hell!"

From a crest they looked across the deeply dissected valleys of the North Platte and the Laramie. A haze that might have been dust or smoke lay on the horizon.

"That could be it," Johnny said. "Twelve thousand longhorns would stir up a bit of dirt."

"Twelve thousand!" José cried. "Saints of my ancestors, then this is the grandfather of all trail herds. Such a herd of cattle will roll over Montana like a flood and pick it as bare as a newborn baby's behind in one season."

"They'll play hell picking Montana bare. Mountains with ice on 'em forty feet thick! Canyons so deep they get only sixteen hours of sunshine in the entire year. Why, stretch the wrinkles out of Montana and I'll wager she'd be bigger'n Texas."

Water holes along Goodings Coulee had been trampled to deep ooze. Afterward, the herd had spread widely to graze, taking the grass along a three-mile swath. The evening breeze from the north carried an odor of droppings, and the oily hides of cattle.

At sunset they crested a low prairie summit and saw the herd scattered by thousands along the river bottoms of the Platte.

Supply wagons, white-sheeted, had been drawn in a half circle in the protection of some squat box-elder trees. Upstream about two miles was a second camp with more wagons. They could hear the "Hi-up! Hi-up!" cries of cowboys still working cattle.

Big Bill said, "I hope we're in time for supper. I'm so hungry I got this horse scared of me."

It was still two or three miles down steplike benches, and twilight was settling. Men still rode, splashing shallow water, roping and dragging mired cattle from the sand-choked river. The carcasses of two beeves hung on a cottonwood limb, skinned out and cooling before being loaded into the cook wagon. Sharp through the dust and cattle smells came the smell of coffee.

40

Bill pulled up at the riverbank and said, "Say, that *is* an outfit."

"It's an outfit when Mixler and the Haltmans change ranges. We better ride in and make our talk before dark. I'd hate to come up sudden and start a herd like that to running."

"Would they run from good water, good grass, over the hill to the desert?" José asked.

"You can't tell when a big herd will run, or where it'll stop. Remember once I was with the Long Seven nursing a big herd along, and we bedded down about three miles from Leesburg, on the bottoms. We were too close to the railroad, as it turned out, because when the train came along and let out a toot, they were up and running, four thousand of 'em all at the same time. Didn't kill anybody, but the whole town was tramped right into the ground so they had to get the railroad surveyors out from Topeka so they could tell where the streets were."

They crossed the river, a treacherous stream with a current broken by mud bars, and dismounted on the north bank to empty their boots and wring dirty water out of their socks.

Apparently their approach had gone unnoticed. Sounds of the camp, now a scant hundred yards away, were deadened by willows and cottonwoods. The smell of coffee was still there, however — coffee mixed with the tang of wood smoke.

They walked, leading their horses, following a crooked trail through brush. Distantly they had glimpses of firelight.

A man suddenly loomed up. He had a rifle in the crook of his arm, angled only slightly downward, his hand through the lever, thumb hooked on the hammer.

"All right, you drifters, stay where y' are."

He had a mildly unpleasant voice. Johnny had noticed that most voices sound unpleasant when they're backed up by the threat of a gun. The man moved a little, coming out of shadow, and they could see him. He was under average height, had a small face with a small mouth and small eyes, but not weak. It was the face of a man who'd been down the long coulee, had taken his knocks, and knew his way.

He looked them over and said, "Don't you know you're liable to get shot, ridin' in like that after dark?"

"Why?" Johnny asked mildly.

He thought for a second and said, "Injun country."

Johnny laughed and said without offense, "Sitting Bull must have his paint spread pretty thin if he's holding all the ground between here and the Little Big Horn."

"The boss says it's Injun country." He'd raised his voice, making it plain that whatever the boss said was right, and that ended the matter.

Johnny said, "Then Injun country it is. All the more reason for giving welcome to three white men. I guess you can use 'em before you get to the Yellowstone."

Their voices had reached through the brush and men were up by the fire, trying to hear.

Someone called, "They strangers, Billy?"

"Yeah. Three of 'em."

"Ask if they're from Willow Creek."

"Where you from?"

"Maverly."

Billy relayed the information and asked, "Where you headed?"

"Here. Is that Mixler yonder?"

He was surprised. "Yeah."

"Then that's our meat. If you or that Winchester neither one got objections, we'll walk yonder and talk with him."

Billy moved and let them by. There were eighteen or twenty men, some of them up and looking, but most of them sprawled around the fire, drinking coffee. One, rangy and powerful, had walked out to meet them. Johnny knew it was Mixler without having to ask. He had "boss" branded all over him.

Mixler kept tilting his head to one side, trying to get a look at them by the poor blending of twilight and firelight. He was thirty-six or thirty-eight years old, his height about six-one. He had a frame that would have accommodated another thirty pounds of weight, but rough living had taken him down, and he probably weighed no more than 180. His trousers were wrinkled toward the crotch from long riding, and they stuck to the insides of his legs. Tom Mace had referred to them as stud-horse legs, and that was a good description. Firelight, striking sidewise across his face, revealed its strong lines, big jaw, prominent nose, high cheekbones. His gun belt, cinched high around his waist, was decorated by half a dozen *conchas* of the type Navajos hammered out of four-bit pieces and sold along the sidewalks at Oro Grande. The *conchas* caught reflection from the fire intermittently as the high flames burst up.

"Mixler?" Johnny said. "I'm called Johnny Colt. These are my friends José Murphy and Bill Spooner."

Mixler met him halfway to shake hands. His eyes had narrowed a trifle, when Johnny gave his name, but he made no comment.

"Looking for jobs?" Mixler asked. "You're welcome to drift along and hit the grub pile, but we're filled up on cowboys."

"You don't understand. We own some of those cattle. The Rocking A. We bought in fifty-one per cent from Tom Mace. He sent us along to take over."

Mixler started to say something and checked himself. For just a moment his face in the long-slanting firelight had become hollow and predatory. His hands moved and came to rest on his hips. The muscles in his shoulders bulged the blue material of his shirt. Then he eased off and decided to laugh.

"You're going to do *what?*"

"Take over the Rocking A end of the herd."

"The hell you are! Tom never mentioned any partners, and he's not here to identify any now. That beef is in my charge, and it'll stay there until he shows up and says otherwise."

"He's in no condition to show up, but we got a paper that should satisfy you." Johnny drew it from his pocket and handed it across. There was no triumph in his manner, he just handed it over. Pretending not to notice the jolted expression on Mixler's face, he ambled

44

to the fire, nudged the pot with his boot toe, and said, "That coffee sure enough smells like Texas."

Some of the boys laughed. They were from Texas and New Mexico, old rebs looking for new pasture, and his accent awoke a kinship among them.

A gangling, gray-whiskered cook in a filthy flour-sack apron stopped wrestling supplies around inside the wagon and said, "Well, help yourself."

"Thanks."

He found a tin cup in the plunder box and poured. The coffee was boiling hot, and so strong it was thick. He blew across its surface, had a swallow of the stuff, and let his eyes rove the men around the fire.

He recognized only one of them, Star Glynn.

Star lay on his side, chewing a blade of grass, smiling a little. He had a round face, bright blue eyes, and an unruly mop of blond hair. He looked to be about twenty-one, but he was older.

"Hello, Star," Johnny said.

"Why, hello, Johnny. I was wondering if you weren't going to recognize me."

Star rolled over and propped himself half off the ground to shake hands.

Johnny said in his half-laughing drawl, "No, I was just surprised to see you here. Punching cows. You were way up in the world last I remembered. Whatever happened to that foreman's job you were holding down for the Three Bar O?"

Star spat out the grass. It seemed to leave a bad taste. "You know what happened to it. My pay ended the same day McCall straightened that rope."

"So they hung Lloyd McCall!"

"You know they did."

"Sure, I knew. But I had nothing to do with it."

"That's because you weren't around." He didn't sound angry. He hadn't cared a damn about McCall. He'd never cared a damn about anybody except Star Glynn.

McCall had operated the Three Bar O, a dark-of-the-moon outfit that dealt in wet horses from both sides of the Rio Grande, peddling them all the way north to the gold camps of Colorado, and Star had ramrodded the spread. He didn't look like a ramrod, with his mild eyes and young face, but he had a pair of supple wrists that could wheel those .45s, and he had a killer's cold lack of emotion that let him pull the triggers no matter what.

"I was some distance off the night they stretched Lloyd." Johnny still talked with a laugh in his voice. "If I'd been there I guess I'd have delayed that hanging along enough to find out about that dapple line-back of mine. I always had an idea that McCall stole him from me."

He came down hard on the name, making it "*McCall* stole him from me," and Star took no offense.

"We had a lot of strays in the bunch." He yawned.

Mixler, with the paper turned toward the fire, had read it all the way through. Now he folded it and handed it back. His face didn't show whether he liked it or not, but he accepted the genuiness of it, and he indicated that with a jerking nod of his head.

46

"All right, Johnny. This is Tom's signature. It's legal. They're his cattle, and if he wants to give half of 'em away, that's his business. Statement says nothing about the rest of his outfit, but I guess that's tossed in. He's got a wagon, a bob-tailed remuda, and a couple ton of supplies. They'll do you all the way to Montana, or, if you like, you can just pool it with us, and eat out of the cook wagon."

Johnny said, "We're not taking 'em through to Montana. We're splitting off up yonder and driving to Deadwood, like Tom planned."

"Wait a minute, Johnny. Has he talked you into doing something he didn't have guts to try himself?"

"Tom has guts enough, I reckon. He just don't set a horse too good."

Mixler gave him a long look. There was amusement in it, and pity. "Three of you, and nine hundred longhorns through the worst stretch of Indian country in the West! How far do you think you'll get before Sitting Bull has your hair and his squaws are stripping your beef for jerky?"

"We'll take that chance, seh."

Mixler drove the heels of his hands together, jerked his head back, and laughed. "Well, maybe. And maybe not. It's easy to take those chances lying here safe and snug on the North Platte, and something else when you get to the Belle Fourche and see the war smoke in the sky. Maybe you'll decide it's better to cut yourself a piece of Montana grass than be a piece of hair on some Cheyenne's lance."

CHAPTER
FIVE

They sprawled on the ground, ate leavings from the stew pot, and drank coffee bitter-strong off the grounds. A cowboy named Pecos played a harmonica while José strummed his guitar and sang.

Johnny Colt talked with Star Glynn, Rasmussen, Evas Williams and Billy Six-Spot. Billy it was who had stopped them with the Winchester; Rasmussen was tall, ungainly, slack-jawed, and smelled of whisky; Evas Williams, no more than twenty years old, carried two guns in a manner identical to Star Glynn's, and copied all his mannerisms.

Johnny lay back with his hat over his eyes, and seemed to be half asleep while discussing some mutual acquaintances down around Mascalero. He kept thinking about Tom Mace, and while the talk was on other things, he had an idea they were thinking about him, too.

Finally Johnny drawled, "I saw Ed Ward and Kiowa in Maverly. They quit the herd?"

He noticed a sudden tension in the bodies of Rasmussen and Billy Six-Spot, but Star was as easy as ever. "They might have. I ain't watching over that pair."

Johnny lay with his eyes almost closed, thinking about the bushwack bullet Tom had taken, and Deadwood seemed a long way off.

As if reading his thoughts, Star asked, "You really think you'll slice such a big chunk of money for yourself in Deadwood?"

"Tom said take 'em to Deadwood. We're takin' 'em."

A man had come down the steps from Haltman's wagon and was looking that way. The coal of his cigarette dimly lit his thin features.

"There's buttons and lace," Evas Williams said with a snigger.

Star Glynn said some small thing that shut him up, but Johnny knew they were in the habit of sneering at the man among themselves.

"That's not Vern Haltman, is it?" Johnny asked.

"Yeah, that's Vern. You know him."

"We met, but it was years ago. He wouldn't remember."

Haltman did remember, though. "You're one of the Colter boys," he said, coming around the wagon at a limp, as though one boot were too tight. There was an unexpected sincerity in the way he spoke and shook hands. Lots of things had changed since old Saltis Haltman, ruling his chunk of Texas, had ordered his family's hats from Germany, boots from Spain, and trousers from England. Johnny had disliked Vern in those days, but now he'd changed. His cocky-kid swagger was all gone, and he seemed beat out by the trail, almost discouraged.

"I didn't think you'd remember me," Johnny said.

Vern Haltman smiled and said, "Some men you don't forget. I recollect you, plain as yesterday, riding in from Humbrite with that forty-four calibre rim-fire pistol you'd won in the raffle. You were just a button of sixteen, but the boys got to joshing you, and wanting to shoot at dollars. Why, when you finished there wasn't tobacco money at the ranch till next payday. Only one man I ever saw could outshoot you, and that was your brother Haps. Whatever happened to him?"

"He was killed in the wah, at Pea Ridge."

"Sorry. I guess I should have known, but there were so many. I lost a couple of brothers, too. I came out all right, with one leg a little shorter than the other, and Ellis and Tommy were too young. Ellis is up at the wagon now, and Lita's somewhere around. She's my half sister. I'd consider it a favor if you'd come up and have a drink with me."

The Haltmans' wagon was a big Conestoga with a sheet-covered "prairie schooner" top. A candle lighted the interior. It was pretty well loaded with supplies, but space had been cleared for eating and sleeping. A table on hinges was folded against the wall. A bed consisting of blankets and a hair mattress was rolled and served as a seat. At the far end was another bed with a strip of tattered curtain that could be let down.

Vern was getting the bottle when someone crawled in by way of the front seat. He was a rusty-haired fellow of twenty-two or twenty-three, much more blunt-featured than Vern, but still similar to him in an indefinable way that stamped them as brothers. He was carrying some saddle gear and a ball of cinch cord.

Vern asked, "Remember my brother Ellis? Ellis, this is Jonathan Colter."

Ellis dumped his load and turned with the old, cocky Haltman manner. "Jonathan Colter? I'd never have known it. I thought you were Johnny Colt."

"I haven't been called Colter three times in the last three years. I guess we both left a lot behind in Texas."

Ellis caught the edge of the remark, and he seemed ready to flare back. Then he checked himself, waited for Vern to bring an extra glass, and drank with them. Vern and Johnny then talked about old friends, and the days when they were kids "befoah the wah," and Ellis, finding himself only half interested, kept hitting the bottle.

Johnny scarcely noticed the passage of time until he felt the wagon weave with a man's heavy weight and knew without looking around that Clay Mixler had come in the back door.

Mixler, bent with his head against the roof sheets, nodded hello and shook his head to Vern's offer of the bottle all in a couple of abrupt movements. His eyes traveled to the curtained-off end of the wagon.

"Where's Lita?" he asked.

Vern looked a trifle thinner and older. He reached for something with a twitch of his fingers, changed his mind. "She's — I don't know where she is."

Johnny knew he was lying, and Mixler knew it. There was an unsteady pause, and it was so quiet they could hear José outside, plucking his guitar, singing:

"Before I'd live a cowboy's life
I'd shoot myself weeth a butcher knife."

Mixler said, "It was about that sorrel mare. She's been wanting to ride her."

Ellis got his mind away from the bottle and said, "Lita? Why, she said she was riding up to see Callie McCrae. Callie had another of her attacks."

Mixler's stiffness dropped from him then. He changed his mind about the drink. He poured a small one and took it with a series of sips, drawing it across his tongue in the manner of a man who drinks because he enjoys the taste of liquor more than its effects.

"That damned howling McCrae woman! Every coulee crossing she has one of her attacks. You ever notice that a woman always aches someplace?"

"Squaws don't," Ellis said.

"No, a buck Injun's too smart. He keeps a squaw at work so she don't have time. White man pampers his women too much."

"Callie's sick," Vern said.

"Eh? Well, *maybe* she is."

Johnny said, "You mean there are *women* in that upper camp?"

Mixler cried bitterly, "Hell, yes! We're a real outfit. Regular damned rolling shantytown. I offer the protection of my outfit through Sioux country, and damned if they don't show up with their women and whelps." He didn't look at Vern as he said it, but still his manner showed that it was Vern Haltman who allowed them to get away with it. "Well, I warned them. I told them it'd be no trip for a woman. I told them I was taking the cattle through by way of the best grass and water, and that their wagons would have to follow the best way they could. Now they'd like to forget about that. They think I'm getting too tough. They're tickful of advice. They tell me I ought to be following that freight road toward the Laramies so it's be easier on their aching backs." He jerked his shoulders with a rough burst of laughter. "To hell with them and their aching backs. We'll bounce some of the tallow off 'em and they won't have so much to ache. I don't give a damn whether they end up in wagons or on foot, or being drug in an Injun travois. I'm following the grass. That's how it is with a trail herd. This is root hog or die."

Vern watched him leave. He moved nervously, and after Mixler rode away he walked to the door of the wagon to look after him.

Thinking of Lita, Johnny said, "Mix has a wife down in Texas, hasn't he?"

"Yeah. She hasn't been living at the ranch. Not for a year. She's not so well."

"She's crazy," Ellis said.

Vern cried with short temper, "No, she isn't!"

"What d'you call it when a woman tries to burn down the house?"

Johnny said, "Maybe she had him inside it."

They all laughed then, and had another drink. Lita would be about seventeen now, Johnny was thinking. Old Saltis Haltman had had her and Tommy by his second wife, that pretty Cherokee half-breed.

"How old is your half brother now?" he asked Ellis.

"Tommy? He's eighteen."

"Older'n Lita?"

"Yes. About a year and a half."

Johnny thought about it while rolling a cigarette and lighting it from the candle. "Let's see. I was nineteen when I got home from the wah. Yeah, that's about right. They were eight or nine years old then." He reached over, ran his fingers through Ellis' bristly red hair, and said, "You weren't much moren' a kid, either, Button," and calling good night to Vern, went outside.

It was a fine, clear night, cool after the intense heat of afternoon, the air slightly moist from the river, filled with the odor of mint and green growth. It all felt good to a man's nostrils after so long on the brown, baked prairie. Johnny Colt filled his lungs a few times, then, avoiding the fire, he walked to the rope corral where the wrangler was holding horses for the night watch. The wrangler was a kid of sixteen or seventeen. He'd injured his foot recently; the side of one boot was cut away, and some dirty bandage leaked out. He limped over, took Johnny's makings, and rolled one.

"Easy night," he said. "Half watch. They been a little spooky, but this good grass and water quieted 'em down. Say, you're Johnny Colt! You were in on that ruckus down at Mascalero, weren't you?"

Johnny wouldn't talk about it. He asked about Tom Mace's saddle string. One of his horses, a big bay, was in the corral.

"Gonzales has been riding him," the wrangler said. "He's one of Haltman's punchers. You can have him, I suppose, or one from the Haltman string. Maybe a couple if you're willing to give up the bay. Vern's pretty good about these things."

"You rope out one of Haltman's, then. I'd like to drift down to the lower camp. Might find somebody I know."

While cutting out and saddling a horse, the wrangler named over the men in the lower camp. "Reavley, he's got the biggest cut of beef, but nothing big as Mixler or Haltman. Then there's McCrae and Jason, they both got families, and old Wolf Carson with maybe fifty head."

Johnny didn't recognize any of the names. They were the owners of haywire outfits that Mixler had picked up on his way north.

He rode carefully through the brush, avoiding the bedded cattle, and found the upper camp asleep except for a Mexican puncher who was cleaning quicksand off his gear.

"How's Mis' McCrae?" he asked, just to say something.

"Seek. Very seek." He slapped his lean middle. "I theenk she don't get better queek she die."

"She's that bad?"

"Eh-sure. A cow herd — thees is no place for woman." He pointed north. "Up there, near Black Hills, I hear the country grows rougher. Pretty soon no wagons, no notheeng. What will she do then?"

Johnny talked with him a while, and by the light of a rising moon looked at the wagons. Most of them were scarred and wobbly-wheeled. A tent, half rags, stood under a box-elder tree. The sound of snoring men came from inside. There were no other sounds.

He said good night in Spanish and started back. A rider had seen him and come to a stop. It was Vern Haltman.

Knowing Johnny had seen him, Vern rode out of the brush.

"How is she?" Vern asked, meaning Callie McCrae.

"Pretty sick, the puncher says. Who's right about her — him or Mixler?"

"I don't know. I guess she's sick, all right."

Vern hadn't been curious about Callie, it was his sister. They found her back at camp talking to Mixler near the dying fire.

She was a small girl, dark and pretty. The high, tight waist of her plain gingham dress accentuated both her slimness and the breadth of her hips. Her hair, divided in two braids, fell to her shoulders. The braids made her look more like an Indian than she would have otherwise, but she was only a quarter-breed.

She caught sight of Johnny's face and kept staring at it.

Vern said, "This is Jonathan Colter, from back in Texas."

She made no sign of hearing him. Fire gave her skin a ruddy cast. It placed a sultry depth in her eyes, and for some reason Johnny remembered that girl back in Texas, not the blonde one, but La Favorita, who danced in the cantina.

Mixler noticed her preoccupation and spoke in a voice that was unexpectedly loud. "Seems like

56

everybody's got the idea of riding at the same time. Don't you get enough of it in the day?"

Johnny said, "We were wondering about the sick woman. I hear she's bad off. Maybe if it's all right with her man, I'll have Big Bill Spooner look at her tomorrow. He's mighty good with sick folks."

Mixler bid good night to Lita and waited for her to go inside the wagon. Then he said in a brittle voice, "I think you boys will have your hands full doing your share of riding on that nine hundred head of beef with out nursing any sick women. I told you she wasn't very bad off. Isn't my word good enough?"

"You're the boss, seh."

Johnny Colt nodded good night to him and prowled around the wagon to where Bill and José had pitched their beds. Neither of them was asleep. They'd been listening to his conversation with Mixler.

Big Bill said in his high-pitched voice, "Gosh, Josie, what do you make of Johnny? I never hear him that polite to anybody. I think that rough, tough grizzly has the fear of damnation thrown into him."

José sat up in his blankets and bowed, imitating Johnny's voice. "You are the boss, seh!"

Johnny said, "You're damned right he's the boss." He pulled off his boots, still wet from the river, and went on in his easy voice. "Facts of life, boys. Art of staying alive in hostile country. Now, I was three years in the army. Tully's Brigade, Cavalry, Army of the Mississippi. You learn a few things in the army. F'instance, you sort of recount yourself after a while and find out you ain't so damned many pennies. They say, 'Do this,' and you do it. When a man's your commander and he says, 'You take that saddle off the horse's back and put it on his belly,' you don't tell him he's crazy, you just go ahead and do it."

"Tully say to do thees? Then I say he was crazy."

"No, he didn't. I'm just trying to drive home a point in terms simple enough for you to understand. Now, a trail herd is like an army. Going through Injun country, it's better to do the wrong thing all together than for everybody to be smart on his own. I'd rather have one middle-class commander than twenty good ones all contraryin' each other's orders. I'm not saying Mixler's not a good boss. In the last go-round a commander is good or not depending on whether he obtains his objective."

Bill said, "Then Grant was better than Lee. He ended up with the whole damned country."

Johnny stopped drying his feet and sat with a stiffened spine. "The armies of Lee, as well as those of Beauregard and Bragg, were successful in attaining each of their military objectives almost to the last. Speaking, seh, from a purely military point of view, the Confed'racy didn't lose the wah. From a military view, the Confed'racy was glorious and triumphant."

"Señor, I have a book, and in thees book —"

"To hell with your book. We won the *wah*. The South was not destroyed by an army, but by a band of brigands, attacking not soldiers, not cannon, not fortresses, but by slaughtering hawgs and chickens and burning cawnfields. Yes, and by killing women and children. Do you call that a *military* exploit?" He got

58

hold of himself then, laughed, and said, "Getting back to Grant and Lee, did you know that during the final campaign of the wah, Grant lost in casualties more men than Lee had in his entire army?"

José said, "You are trying to tell *me*, from Mexico, about the science of war? In one hundred years how many civil wars had your country?"

"Only one, thank God."

"*One!* In Chihuahua each odd-numbered year is fought the civil war."

"Little two-bit wars."

"Well, those are the most fun. And you made mention of casualties. How many had your General Lee? Feefty thousand? One hundred thousand? Let me tell you of my uncle, Ramón Telesforo Julio Aldasoro de Santillo y García, we call him Ray for short, he is general wccth medal from Santa Ana saying Caballero de la Libertad. Did your Lee have such a medal? Answer me."

Johnny had heard the story many times before. Wearily he said, "No."

"No. So I will tell you about thees one campaign. For one hundred days, on Rio Conchos, fighting every day it was not too hot, maneuvering every step like Napoleon, did my uncle lose five hundred men? Did he lose one hundred men?"

"He lost one man," said Johnny.

"*Sí*. On the last day of thees magnificent campaign did this one soldier, this miserable peon, allow himself to be bitten by the gila monster. My uncle, the general, he was furious. Thees man he would have shot at sunrise for breaking his record, but alas, he was already dead."

"Oh, hell!" Johnny said. "You take the first watch."

CHAPTER
SIX

They awoke at gray dawn. The vinegar-tempered cook, nicknamed Daddy Bearsign, was banging a tin pan, threatening to feed the breakfast to the wolves.

No one took his ease at breakfast. Coffee was drunk standing, scalding hot. There were pans of hot bread, and beef fried and boiled up in a brown gravy. Cowboys kept galloping into camp, and Daddy Bearsign kept cursing them for kicking dirt in his cook pans.

The Mexican flunky got the horses hitched before half the crew had eaten.

"Git that grub down. This is no time for table manners," Daddy Bearsign kept shouting. "That herd's already on the move and I got a steep trail to pull. By grab, if I don't get out o' here you'll have dirt and cow hair for dinner."

The meat wagon was already on its way. The Haltmans' wagon, with young Tommy in the high spring seat, followed it. A low-wheeled supply wagon belonging to Tom Mace was next. Daddy Bearsign stopped shouting, tossed his cook pans inside, and shouted, "Git going!" to the flunky up front, holding the reins.

The wagon went careening across the hummocky bottoms while longhorns got out of the way, snorting and walleyed. Men were still eating. They finished, washed plates and cups in the river, and rode at a gallop to toss them in the plunder box. Lead steers were already climbing the steep northern bluffs, and Daddy Bearsign had to get ahead of them and drive hard to the noon camp site.

Cattle milled in the brush with cowboys swinging goads to drive them out; cattle moved up the bluffs in tight columns, digging streams of dirt and clouds of dust. Above, on the flat prairie, lead cattle by habit forged in front and others followed, while the hoof-sore and laggard formed the drag.

The big herd was formed of several small herds, and their paths would diverge until sometimes a mile separated them. The air was filled with dust and bawling. The sun rose and shone ruddy-hot through dust. Cowboys rode with their hats down, their neckerchiefs raised against the dust, and drove the laggards with a continual "Hi-ya! Hi-ya!"

The wagons from Mixler's camp rolled straight ahead, over the bulge of the prairie, down miles of gentle descent and up again, leaving the herd behind. Other wagons followed, more heavily laden, less pressed for time, trying to find a road free of the bumpety-bump of bunch grass.

Johnny saw the girl and rode across to intercept her.

"How's Mrs. McCrae?" he asked.

She shook her head. "She's in bed on the floor. The jouncing around is hard on her."

"Is she really sick?"

"Yes!"

"I'm sorry. I just asked. You hear things."

"Who told you she wasn't?"

He didn't want to drag in Mixler's name. "Why doesn't McCrae turn back to Maverly?"

"And then what? They haven't a dime. No, they're going on to Montana."

"That's not heaven, either, you know."

She sat with hands propped fore and aft on her side-saddle and swung her body around on its slim waist to look at the prairie. It seemed level from a distance, but bunch grass and the washed-out depressions between had turned it into a teamster's hell.

"I wish there were a smoother way. It'd be so much easier for all of them if we hit the freight road."

"That's thirty miles west."

"I know. Maybe we'll be there in four or five days. We'll have to swing west around the Willow Springs." Then she asked, "How is Tom Mace?"

"Doing well enough. What happened to him, anyhow?"

She cried defensively, "You can bet the Haltmans had nothing to do with it!"

"Why, I didn't guess they did."

During the heat of afternoon, atop the high prairie, the herd was allowed to spread and graze through a good area of grass and sage. That night they camped at a shallow sinkhole lake. The herd was restless. The sky blackened and there was a dry rain — wind, lightning, and eddies of dust, with the stars out from one horizon to the other when it was time for the middle watch.

Few of the cattle had drunk their fill. They were up early, moving west of north. Mixler's point riders immediately swung them to a direction slightly east of north.

He was shaping a course toward Willow Creek. At noon the small ranchers bunched their wagons and had a powwow about it.

"What's the trouble with 'em?" Johnny Colt asked Big Bill, who rode over from that way.

"They figure we ought to head west, toward the Laramies."

"Do they want water and grass, or are they just interested in a nice, smooth road?"

Daddy Bearsign stood in the wagon with his shapeless hat down over his eyes, chawing and spitting and looking off at the other cluster of wagons.

"There goes Mixler," he grunted, more to himself than to anyone else. "Look at that backbone on him. Blow the marrow out of that backbone and you could use it for a rifle bar'l. By grab, that Dave Jason's going to push him too far one o' these days and he'll be needing help to chew gravy. Mix will knock his teeth down his throat, wager gold money he will."

Bill Spooner asked, "Think there'll be trouble?"

"I don't give a damn about the trouble Jason makes for himself. All I'm worried about is if the coffee will hold out to Miles."

Johnny said, "If there's a meeting, I guess those nine hundred steers give us an excuse to get in on it."

He rode over with Big Bill and found a group of nine men gathered beyond one of the old Conestoga wagons.

Mixler had dismounted and stood in his favorite spread-legged manner, listening while someone talked in a brassy, nasal voice.

A heavy-set woman in her early thirties stood in the back door of the Conestoga, shading her eyes with her forearm. She looked excited and scared. As he rode by, Johnny noticed that there were a couple of half-grown boys in the shadow of the canvas top behind her.

The man's brassy voice was saying, "That's what we should have done back at the North Platte. Well, it's not too late. We can turn west, and by dry-camping one, two nights we can still get to the Sulphur Water."

"That Dave Jason?" Johnny asked, and Big Bill nodded.

Jason was thickset and powerful, with the hands and arms of a blacksmith. A crop of black whiskers disguised his age, but he was probably between thirty-five and forty. Mixler and Vern Haltman were there, but he'd turned his back on them and was addressing his words to the members of his own camp — the small owners, Reayley, McCrae, Wolf Carson and Fred Jardine.

Big Bill said, "There's Star Glynn."

Without turning, Johnny asked, "Where?"

"Sittin' a horse beyond that Pittsburgh wagon."

Johnny grinned without humor. "Kid Bushwhack!"

"You think he's yellow?"

"No, he's not yellow. He's got guts to face any man on earth with those sixes of his, only if there's a safer way he'll take it."

Johnny could tell that Mixler was furious. His eyes were narrowed to slits, and his face seemed to be all jawbone.

"You through?" he shouted at Jason.

Jason went on, shouting even louder than Mixler, saying over the things he'd said already. Mixler waited, trying to keep a rein on his fury until Jason talked himself out.

"Dave!" he said, forcing his voice down. "Dave, you've been finding a lot of fault with the way I've run this outfit lately."

Jason spat tobacco juice explosively. "Let's not make it personal. I got nothing agin *you*." He cast one powerful arm at the herd. "But I got four hundred and twenty cattle out there, and outside of that busted old wagon and four head of draught stock, it's all in the world I own. You say go to Willow Creek? It's fenced and they sell the water. I got no money to pay. I'm tradin' none of my cattle for it, either. I say we ought to go west, same way as the other herds."

"Listen, Dave —"

"Well, that's what I say. We should have headed northwest at the Medicine. I could see their trail there plain as day."

"Listen, Dave. I've taken this all for the last time. I never told you that before, Dave, but this time I am. This is the *last time*. You signed up with the understanding I was captain. You signed up to do as I said. Dave, that's what you're going to do."

"A man can go just so far on a thing like that. I'm through and McCrae's through. We're heading —"

"All right. I'll give that point. You and McCrae can go or stay. But your cattle go with the herd."

Jason's fists were doubled, his shoulders sloped forward. He had heavy eyebrows, and he seemed to be trying to peer through them into Mixler's face as he said hoarsely, "No, I'm cutting my stock. I'm —"

Moving with a quickness unexpected in a man of his size, Mixler came forward, feinting slightly with his left hand. Jason moved, tossing both arms, and tossing them too high. The left side of his face was unprotected, and Mixler's right fist came up with the stunning impact of a sledge.

Jason's head snapped back so hard his hat flew off. His eyes were jarred, with a distant look in them. He tried to keep his balance, but his legs bent beneath him and he sat down.

He didn't quite reach the ground. Mixler, who had reined in his rage too long, now had lost all control of himself. He leaped forward, grabbed the heavy-set man by the front of his shirt, held him up on his limber legs, and smashed him three times with vicious short hooks.

He got a deep breath. He still held Jason up. Jason's hair, long uncut, hung over his eyes. His mouth was open. But Mixler still wasn't finished. With deliberation he drew back his fist and drove still another blow to Jason's jaw.

Johnny heard a curse from Bill Spooner. The big fellow started around him, but Johnny moved and hipped him off balance. Bill pivoted, still trying to get around, but Johnny had him by the gun belt.

"Stay here."

"Damn it, I ain't —"

"Stay here!"

This time a note in Johnny's voice stopped him.

Mixler held Jason up until some of the grogginess left him. He said, "Dave, don't try it again. Dave, listen. I'd have killed you if it hadn't been for your woman and kids." He dumped Jason to the ground, gave his pants a hitch, and looked around. "All of you haven't got wives and kids," he said.

One of Jason's boys, an eleven-year-old called Nubbins, darted down from the wagon and lifted his father's head out of the dirt. Blood ran from Jason's mouth. It mixed with sweat and dirt and whiskers and trickled down his neck. Nubbins, still holding his father's head, looked up at Mixler with hate in his eyes.

"You dirty killer. You bushwacker. That's what you are, a bushwhacker. We know what you're tryin' to do. Everybody does. You're tryin' to bust our outfits and drive us off so you can get to Montana with every hoof claimed in your own book. First it was Tom Mace, and now it's Paw."

His mother came running and cried, "Nubbins, shut up!" She was afraid Mixler would kill him.

"I won't." He was bawling. "Maybe nobody else here got the nerve to tell off this dirty yella-gutted son, but I have. They'da killed old Tom if we hadn't hid him. Then when he got away, that bushwhacker sent Ed Ward and that Kiowa half-breed —"

Mixler had been taken off balance by the sudden outpouring. One big hand froze on the butt of his gun. The fist of his other hand was doubled, but he stood, hearing him. He took two steps forward while the kid refused to retreat. There he'd have driven the sole of his boot to Nubbins' chest, but the kid was too quick for him. He rolled and snaked himself out of the way while still crying and saying, "You dirty bushwhack son!"

Men got between them. Breathing hard through his nostrils, Mixler said, "Get that button out of here or him being a kid won't save him."

Tall, redheaded Rio Reavley got Nubbins by both shoulders and shook him until he stopped talking. "Nubbins, keep our mouth shut! Nubbins!"

Jason was up. He staggered and rubbed a hand back and forth across his eyes. Mixler waited. He waited until he could speak without a tremble of fury in his voice, then he said to the camp in general:

"I got no objections to talking things over with you men, listening to your suggestions and taking them under consideration. I got no objection to your asking why I do things. I'll tell you why I didn't turn west at the Medicine, or at the North Platte. Because we'd lose three days getting to Montana. Three days doesn't sound like much, but three here and three someplace else mounts up. It might give the Lawson herd or Bob King's outfit the first chance at Deergrass range. And nobody's beating me to the Deergrass. Not your sick women, not your broken-down wagons." He cast an arm toward the north. "And not that bunch of lousy Kansas squatters who think they can fence off the only decent water between here and the Niobrara and use it to irrigate spuds."

Rio Reavley let the kid go and said, "They'll make a fight for it if we try to water the herd, Mix. That'll hold us up more'n any three days."

"That remains to be seen." He regarded Reavley with his eyes once more closed to narrow slits. "How about it, Rio? You haven't got any ideas about running the outfit, have you? I hope you don't. You're a damned good man."

"I ain't afraid of you." There was no bravado in it. He wasn't saying it because there were men listening and he wanted to save his pride. He was just stating the fact. He looked first at Mixler, then at Vern Haltman, and then at Star Glynn, who was leaning against a high wagon wheel, one heel in the spokes, his thumbs in his crossed cartridge belts. "And I ain't afraid of your gunmen, either. I knew about you and about them before I signed up, so I got no kick coming. I'll drift along with you. That don't mean I'll like it, but I'll drift with you."

Nobody else spoke. Mixler turned and saw Johnny Colt. "Oh, hello, Johnny. I was going to send for you. Mind riding ahead with Vern and me? Rio, maybe you better come, too. We'll go over and see if we can talk reason to those nesters at Willow Creek. You can't tell, maybe they'll say, 'Come on, boys, and drive your longhorns right through'."

70

CHAPTER
SEVEN

Willow creek lay half a day's ride to the north. There were six of them who went on ahead of the herd. In the lead were Mixler and Johnny Colt, next came Vern Haltman and Reavley, and farther back were Glynn, Rasmussen, and Evas Williams. They got their first view of the green creek bottoms about two hours before sundown.

A heavy rail drift fence had been built to shut the valley off from the northward press of Texas cattle. Lighter fences cut the bottoms up in polygonal-shaped fields, some grayish from the plow, others green with early crops. Directly below, across the valley, was a cluster of log snacks, sheds, and corrals. A half-completed log house stood upstream by a bend, sheltered by cut banks.

"Ever been here before?" Mixler asked Johnny Colt.

"No."

Mixler kept looking along the valley, thinking, rubbing the hard bristle of whiskers along his jaw. "The sweetest water in Wyoming hogged by a hoeman Yankee army. And they'll have the law behind 'em.".

Star said, "A long way behind them. I haven't noticed any law since we left Cheyenne."

Mixler laughed with little sound but a hard jerk of head and shoulders. "Point well taken. Fact, I've noticed none since we left Texas." He pointed east and west. "That settlement covers nine or ten miles. I got a description of it from that peddler we met at Warfeather Springs. Like a closer look, though. Not all of us. Even a yellow Yank sodbuster is likely to get dangerous if you scare him. You stay here, this side of the fence. Johnny and I will go down there and see what we can talk up."

Johnny Colt and Mixler rode down, stirrup to stirrup. As they approached the fence they could hear the tincan rattle of a cowbell. There was no other movement.

"They'll be watching us," Johnny said. "They'll be sure to have the herd spotted."

Mixler said, "Damn their yellow guts, I never thought I'd see the day when I'd be talking to trash-Yankees with my hat in my hand."

"You won't have your hat in your hand."

Mixler smiled, showing his strong teeth. "Well, maybe I won't."

The drift fence was made of heavy cottonwood posts and rails, anchored deeply, set atop the cut banks north of the valley. They skirted it, crossing feeder gullies choked with brush, and came to a big, counterbalanced gate.

Johnny opened it without dismounting, and they rode through.

"Gun shine," Mixler said, his eyes on a creek crossing three or four hundred yards away.

"Field glasses."

"Well, maybe. Want to bet there's not a gun behind them?"

They rode across the bottoms, between wagon tracks, beneath the cool shade of cottonwoods. Some late roses were still out, filling the air with fragrance. The ground was soft from dampness, deeply rutted where wagons had been mired. The creek flowed slowly, wide and shallow.

"There he is," Mixler said without turning his head.

A man was waiting, hunkered in the concealment of a fence corner. They pretended not to see him until he stood up, a Henry rifle in the crook of his arm. He was a weather-beaten man of middle years and middle size, dressed in shapeless clothes.

"Good evenin'," Mixler said. "I don't think you'll be needing that gun."

He tried to talk civilly, but he wasn't a good actor, and there was no hiding the contempt he felt for a sodbuster.

The man didn't point the gun, but he still kept it across his arm.

"Where you headed?" He was frightened, and that made him sound more unfriendly than he intended.

"You don't sound very cordial. That the way things are done back in Kansas?"

"Where you headed?" the man repeated, an unsteady note in his voice.

"Here, I guess, if this is Willow Creek. We're from the trail herd yonder."

The sodbuster kept licking his lips. His eyes traveled repeatedly to the six-guns on their hips, to the new-model Winchester center-fire rifles in their saddle scabbards. He must have known that he didn't stack up against them very well with that old rim-fire Henry.

Mixler said, "We were wanting to bring our cattle through here for water, but we didn't want trouble, either. That's why we came down here — to talk about it."

"I ain't got anything to say about it."

"You claim this ground, don't you?"

"Yes, but the association, it's up to them. I got nothing to say about it. I couldn't let you through here if I wanted."

"Well, how do I talk to this association?"

"It'd take a little while. You'd have to gather the men. Some of 'em are gone."

"How many are gone?"

"I don't know. Anyhow, you couldn't get everybody together for a couple of days."

Mixler laughed with a bitter jerk of his shoulders and kept looking at him. The man was still scared. His eyes showed it, and the grip he had on his rifle showed it. A corral and a shed or two could be seen through the trees. Someone else was posted there. His woman, probably, or some of his kids.

Mixler said, "We got a herd of thirsty cattle yonder. Do you think we can sit around two days while you're getting your parliamentary procedure ironed out?"

"Most all the herds go west by way of Sulphur Water."

"Why?"

He didn't know what to answer. Mixler rode on and stopped in the middle of the creek. It was running well, and deep as the knees of his horse.

"I don't see why in hell they'd have to go all the way to Sulphur Water. There seems to be water here."

The man cried, "We ain't letting any trail herds through. It ain't the water. It's our crops. A big herd would tramp half our crop into the ground. If we had the crops took in —"

"Thanks. We'll be back in October." He hooked his thumb at a fenced-off turnip patch up the rise. "You got papers for that ground? What right you have to fence off public domain?"

The hoeman didn't answer. He'd let Mixler and Johnny Colt get at such wide angles that he couldn't watch both of them at the same time. He started edging along the fence.

A woman then came into sight, toting a long, muzzle-loading double gun. She cried, "Yes, we got papers for it. We got U.S. government papers. We own it under the Veteran's Act."

Mixler's lips formed the words, You damned Yankees! but he set his teeth against saying them aloud. When he spoke, he said, "Well, Missus, you got something better'n any Union gov'ment papers there in your hand. Anyhow, we're not here to make trouble. If we were, we wouldn't come down here like this, just the two of us. We want to talk water. If our herd tramps some spuds, why, we'll pay for 'em. Cheyenne prices. Maybe we'd pay something whether they tramped anything or not."

She cried, "We heard that from Texas men before."

Mixler dug in his pants pockets and took out five twenty-dollar gold pieces. He spread them in his palm. "Would these pay for a few turnips, ma'am?"

It was more money than this family would see in a year.

He went on, "Now, let's not be foolish. We can help each other. You take us to the head man in your association before we *do* drift for Sulphur Water."

They waited while the hoeman caught a spavined old work horse, put a blind bridle on him, and mounted bareback. He had no place for the Henry gun, so he carried it in one hand in front of him.

The woman now ran out and cried, "Paw, you be careful!"

"I'll be all right. I see Clint and Buster coming."

She still didn't like his riding away. Johnny Colt looked back an instant before the house was hidden from view. She stood there, shading her eyes with her forearm, a couple of hungry-looking kids watching from a step or two behind.

They rode a quarter mile and saw the two men he'd referred to as Clint and Buster waiting in a grove of cottonwoods. They were sodbusters in patched and faded clothes. Buster, a big, blunt fellow of twenty, had an old double-barreled horse pistol strapped around his waist. Clint, who looked remarkably like him but was more than twice his age, carried a shotgun. Clint was bareback, but the young fellow had an old Union cavalry saddle.

The hoeman didn't bother with introductions. "Where's Hank?" he asked.

"Yonder at the house," Buster said. "Ride over this way a second, will you?"

Mixler said, "Damn it, we haven't got all evening. Take me to this Hank, whoever he is, and talk your private affairs afterward."

Buster's eyes kept traveling to the northern cut banks. He'd seen Star and the others over there and wanted to pass the warning along.

"They're our men," Mixler said. "We rode down here, just the two of us, so nobody would have an excuse to get scared."

Buster stuck out a big underlip. He didn't look very bright. He said, "I'm not scared!"

"I don't wonder, with that cannon you're carrying. I'll bet that thing won the Mexican wah."

Without further talk they were taken around one bend after another to a two-story log house, undoubtedly the proudest structure on Willow Creek. It was sundown then, and men had started to gather. More kept coming after Mixler and Johnny Colt were inside, sitting at a big, rough-board table, drinking bitter black coffee, dickering over the price of water.

Hank Wellens, a fox-faced man of fifty, did all the talking for the Willow Creek settlers. They didn't "pre-suppose" to sell water, he said. Water was a "blessing of Gawd" in this dry country and should be free to all. All they wanted was payment in advance for the damage that would be done to their crops. He named a price of five cents a head.

After a quarter hour of fruitless arguing, trying to beat down the price, Mixler banged the table with his fist, laughed, and said:

"Wellens, you're too much for me. 'Never dicker with a Yankee' — that's sure the truth. Five cents it is. For three thousand head, that's a hundred and fifty dollars."

"We estimate you got considerable more than three thousand head."

Mixler wanted to reach across the table and strangle this Yankee sodbuster who was naming him a liar, but instead he forced a laugh and said, "All right, Wellens, you have me again. I'll tell you the truth — I don't know how many head there are myself. You have your men at that main gate to tally. You have three men and I'll have three men. I'll be there to pay you five dollars for each hundred as they go through."

"Gold."

"In gold." He clumped to the door as men, silent and suspicious, made room for him.

Wellens followed, saying, "They got to come through easy! Thirsty cattle are hard to hold. I'll have my men there, and if you don't keep aholt of that stock there'll be trouble. I won't have 'em rolling over our fields. Fair warning — we'll shoot the first steer that breaks a fence!"

"I'll pay for the damage."

Mixler cursed under his breath all the way back to his horse. Mounted, and riding back toward the gate, he spoke:

"Five cents a head! Five cents to water your cows on the public domain. That's how a yellow Yankee government treats a man."

"Seh, I'm not sure I'm able to pay a nickel a head for my nine hundred. That'd be forty-five dollars, and if there's damage; as there's bound to be —"

"You can pay it as well as I can!" he said with a bitter laugh. "Johnny, let's not worry about that nickel now."

CHAPTER
EIGHT

"How'd you make out?" Reavley asked, riding up through the twilight when they got back through the drift fence.

"Why, first rate. We can water all the cows we like. One bellyful of water, five cents. Figure up the damages."

"I haven't got a hundred dollars cash to my name."

"I'll tell you what I told Johnny — don't worry about it. I'll talk to 'em again."

Star Glynn asked, "How many guns they got to back up that nickel-a-head price?"

"They got some men, and they got some guns, but neither of them looked like a hell of a lot to me, Johnny, did you notice the muzzle on that old Henry the hoeman was packing? Wager a bullet would go down that shot-out barrel rattling like a set of Coahuila castanets."

Reavley kept cursing about the five-cents-a-head price. "You can't get it from people that ain't got it. You know where McCrae's last jag of grub came from? From *me*. I lent 'em twenty dollars back at Ogalalla —"

"You don't like it, then! Well, I don't like it either. I told you I'd try to get a better deal."

It was long after dark when they got back to the herd. The cattle were slow in bedding down. They kept up a steady, thirsty bawling.

"You tell your boys what happened," Mixler said to Reavley.

Daddy Bearsign still had the grub hot for them. Mixler turned his horse over to the wrangler and limped toward his wagon. He called to Johnny Colt, "Come here a second, will you?"

Mixler had a couple of big Conestogas, both loaded with supplies, though in one he'd cleared a space big enough for his bed. He felt around beneath the wagon sheets, pulled out a quart of whisky, handed it over.

"So you haven't got forty-five dollars to pay," he said.

"I might raise it, but I don't want to."

Mixler laughed, waited for the bottle, and drank. He slapped the cork back. "They'll lower their price."

"I doubt they will, seh. Waterin' this herd would destroy a third part of everything they got planted in the bottoms."

Mixler still smiled, but his eyes had narrowed. "What's wrong, Johnny? You afraid of those sodbuster guns?"

"I ain't afraid of 'em. I just don't go out o' my way looking for a fight. Is that why you called me over here, to ask me that?"

"No. I wanted to know what you had against me."

"Nothing, seh."

"What'd Mace say when he signed those steers over to you? Did he say I tried to bushwhack him?"

"Why, I'll tell you what he said. He said Kiowa and Rasmussen tried to bushwhack him. He said he knew too much about some Missouri Pacific mail-car robbery."

"Oh." Some of the suspicion seemed to go out of him. His manner became confidential. "You'll never know how I been fighting to keep this outfiit from splitting down the middle. There's two bunches here. There's the Haltmans and me, and there's that bunch of haywire outfits at the upper camp. You're going to have to choose between us. I think you made your choice already. Which is it going to be?"

Speaking slowly, meeting Mixler's eyes, he said, "I'm like Rio Reavley. I knew you were captain of the herd when I signed up. I knew who you were. I'd heard of you down in Texas. I knew, and I was still willing to take your orders as far as the herd is concerned — from here all the way to the Belle Fourche. That answer your question?"

There was no slight hint of a smile on Mixler's lips now. His eyes were like pieces of gray quartz above his high cheekbones. "Yes," he said, "I guess it does."

The herd was unusually quiet. It was a bad sign. Johnny lay in his blankets, staring at the stars, listening. He could hear night herders making their rounds, singing the endless words of a trail song. He had the feeling that any unexpected sound, or less than that, even the absence of an expected sound would start them up and running.

José came in after riding the first watch, and awoke Big Bill to take over.

"I'll ride the last one tonight," Johnny said.

He fell asleep, and awakened at grub call in the morning. Bill had ridden straight through.

"Why didn't you let me stand my watch?" he asked.

"Hell, there was nothing to watch. Those steers were up, pawin' and movin,' before two o'clock."

The herd, through rising layers of dust, rolled northward, topped the low ridge during hot afternoon, and, bawling for water, were milled to a stop half a mile from the Willow Creek fence.

With steady curses, Daddy Bearsign emptied stale water from his barrel into the coffeepot, which he suspended over a sagebrush fire. Eight or nine men had gathered for grub. Mixler wasn't there. None of the Haltmans were there.

"What the hell's going on here tonight?" Daddy kept saying.

Four men led by Rio Reavley rode down from the other camp. Daddy, wiping sweat from his eyebrows, looked up and said, "If you're looking for water, you can go down to the creek and dip it."

Rio said, "Where's Mix?"

"He don't come around and ask my p'mission to go here or there. Guess that's because I'm nothing but a cook."

Vern Haltman had seen them arrive and rode up at a gallop. "You looking for Mixler? He's down in the valley making a dicker."

"Oh." Rio relaxed a little. He edged his bay bronc close enough so he could look down in the coffeepot. It had just started to boil.

Daddy said, "Well, git down and have yourselves a cup. I'll have beef and doughgod, maybe. And gravy thickened with trail dust. What a hell of a place to camp, right behind this herd. I'd like to know where everybody is. They're generally like a band of wolves this time of night."

Rio and the rest were dismounted, drinking coffee, when Mixler came. His eyes dwelt for a moment on Reavley, on the purple-bruised face of Dave Jason.

He barked to Daddy Bearsign, "Put out that fire. Get the wagon hitched." Rio started to say something, but Mixler's raw voice cut him off. "Go back and get your outfits ready to roll."

Rio said, "What, the hell —"

"We're moving across — tonight."

"How about those nesters? You come to terms with 'em?"

"I told you I'd take care of everything. They'll get paid off. They'll get paid off what they deserve."

Daddy Bearsign cursed and kicked the coffeepot over, putting out the fire. The air was suddenly dark with steam and smoke rising from the blackened sage stalks. Still cursing, Daddy started to hurl things inside the wagon.

Mixler rode off; Reavley and the others rode off, too.

The air was lifeless. Bullet-colored clouds had climbed over the western horizon. There was sheet lightning and distant thunder — the regular nightly dry rain.

Johnny Colt rode along the massive rail drift fence. He met Rasmussen and Evas Williams.

"Where's Mix?" he said to Evas.

"I don't know."

But he did, and his manner advertised it.

Johnny found the remuda, roped a fresh horse. He rode on and met Big Bill Spooner.

"I don't like it," Bill said. "I saw Mix up at the wagon. He had that mean lobo look about him. He's looking for trouble."

"They're looking for trouble, too. Anybody, that fences off water in this country is looking for trouble."

"I don't like it!" Bill repeated. "You said yourself there were women and kids down there."

"They'll have 'em out of harm's way." He didn't sound too sure of it. Bill started to say something more, and Johnny cried, "Damn it, don't squawk to me. I'm not the trail boss here. I just take orders like everybody else."

Riders on the big circle had kept the herd on the gently sloping hillside. It wasn't easy with the smell of water so close below. The thunder was disquieting. It put an electric charge in the air. Waiting became taut, like a string drawn more and more tightly. One big brindle steer, somewhat downhill from the others, bawled in a steady, high-pitched trumpet.

A rider came up from the darkness, shadowy and small. It was Lita Haltman. She drew up with one of her slim movements and said, "Oh, I thought you were Vern."

Johnny wondered if she expected Vern or Mixler. He had no reason to suspect her — only Vern's actions that first night. He could barely make out the smooth outline of her face. Her hair, unbraided tonight, fell in heavy masses around her shoulders. For a few seconds she sat quite straight, her dark eyes on him.

Johnny asked her, "What's Mixler got up his sleeve?"

"How would I know what he's up to?" The sharp defensiveness of her voice was a surprise after the long quiet. "I haven't talked to Mixler since morning."

Johnny tilted his head at the valley, now an uncertain mass of shadow. "Reckon he's yonder, closing the deal?"

"I said I hadn't —"

"Sure."

His questions concerning Mixler had angered her. She touched her heel to the side of her horse and started away, intending to go around the herd on the downhill side, but a rider came up at a stiff jog and spoke to her.

"That you, miss?" It was Billy Six-Spot. "You better get back to the wagon. Vern's looking for you."

Billy rode off with her. The herd quieted. Even the brindle steer had stopped trumpeting.

Suddenly, from up the slope, came the sound of a galloping horse and the clang-clang of a tin pan being drawn on the end of a lariat rope.

The next instant, as though moved by a common mind, the great herd got to its feet and stampeded.

It had been done deliberately, done at Mixler's order.

The earth vibrated. It was like thunder but multiplied a thousand times. Going downhill, the dark sea of cattle split around a little knoll and rejoined, a maddened, bawling mass.

Johnny and Bill Spooner were caught between one end of the herd and the heavy rail fence. They spurred forward, got clear, and swung back. Dust made the air too thick to breathe. In the darkness, it was like a black fog. They sucked air through folded kerchiefs, guided themselves by sound.

A breeze sprang up, carrying the dense layer of dust away from them. Lightning kept flashing closer, and there were big droplets of rain. They could see them dimly.

The lead steers, outdistancing the others by a hundred yards, had been turned by the heavy rail fence. For a few seconds they milled. Men were below, in the bottoms, shooting. Through the dust the powder flames were ruddy, out of focus. Then the main herd bore down, swept the lead steers and fence before it, washed in a dark wave across the valley.

The sound of the herd then seemed far away. They could hear the shouts of teamsters getting the wagons rolling.

José found them. They fell in with other riders. Ahead of them was the cook wagon, bounding wildly across the rough prairie as Daddy Bearsign stood and whipped the team. The Haltman wagon was at his left. Supply wagons followed. Farther away, approaching at an angle, were the wagons from the other camp.

A group headed by Star Glynn galloped upvalley and was turned by a burst of gunfire. The riders swung away and came back in a wild charge, whooping and shooting.

Opposition faded in front of them. Johnny Colt could hear them crashing their horses back and forth through the brush. A voice he recognized as Andy Rasmussen's kept shouting, "Hey, you lousy sodbusters, come on out and collect your money!"

He rode through the dust, among straggling steers, across the bottoms. The herd had taken every fence before it. The boundaries of the fields had been obliterated under the wash of trampling hoofs. He remembered the position of a spud patch, but now there was only dirt, pulverized as though the field had been replowed and harrowed ten times over.

He reached the herd. It made a solid mass along the creek. It spread along the bottoms, still trampling fields, bawling, hunting for water.

He could no longer smell the green things and the late roses — there was only the smell of hide, hair, and manure.

He rode along the herd, found an opening where a stretch of north-south rail fence still stood, and crossed the creek.

A light was burning through the trees. It came from the hoeman's shack. He cut across to it. The hoeman and his family were gone. Some cowboys had lighted the candle and were frisking the larder. There'd been a fire in the stove, and water boiling in a kettle. The woman had been there only a few minutes before.

The boys made tea. A redheaded kid named Pinky Sallards had found one of the woman's poke bonnets and had it on. Mixler rode up, leaned over, and looked inside. He didn't laugh. He barked, "Put that stuff back. We're not robbing 'em. We're just watering the herd."

There was still shooting above and below, but Mixler didn't pay the least attention. The gunman crew he'd put together down on the Red was taking care of things. He kept riding back and forth, shouting to the cowboys, telling them to keep the cattle together, to keep driving the lead one out of the water, to give the next thousand a chance.

Hours later the first portion of the herd commenced moving reluctantly toward the bluffs. José and Al Geppert came up, José walking and a dead man over the back of his horse.

Sight of the limp body swinging stopped the voices of every man at the shack.

"Who is he?" Vern Haltman asked.

José said, "Who knows? A sodbuster, I suppose. The man whose home thees was before we trampled it into the earth."

Mixler heard him and came riding up. "What's that you were saying?"

"They asked who he was. I said he was the man whose home we trampled for one night's water, to save three days on the way to Montana."

Mixler had reared back in his old ramrod posture, his hand ready for the gun at his right hip. José was as slack and apparently off guard as he'd been that night he faced Slavin at the Dublin at Maverly.

Johnny Colt took a long stride, grabbed José by the left arm, and swung him around. "All right, Josie, it's too bad we can't bring him back to life."

"Let me go!" He breathed through clenched teeth from the effort of trying to twist away. "What is wrong with you? Are you yellow inside? *I* am not yellow inside, señor."

Mixler was reining his horse, trying to get at him.

Johnny cried, "Keep away from him, Mix!"

Mixler checked himself, but his face looked hollow, the way it did that day he struck Dave Jason; his legs were rammed hard in the stirrups; his hand was on his six-gun ready to draw.

He met Johnny's gaze and changed his mind. There was no fear in him, he just didn't want the fight to go that far. "All right, but keep him away from me. I'm not taking any lip from a smart Mex."

He issued some commands and rode off. There was still intermittent shooting. Movements of the cattle became a steady push across the bottoms. They had their bellies full of water; the lucky ones had grabbed a few mouthfuls of green grass or potato tops. Docile after the night's stampede, they followed the lead steers up the northern bluffs.

Wagons, with barrels filled, rolled up from the creek, mingling with cattle, hunting a treacherous, zigzag path to the rim. At dawn the settlers launched an attack, but it wasn't a determined one, and they retired. A cowboy named Curly Phelps had taken a bullet through, his thigh and had his horse shot from under him. There were no other casualties.

Reaching the crest, José looked back at the desolated center of the valley while waiting for Johnny Colt. A long accumulated anger lay in his eyes. "What the hell,

Johnny, have you lost your guts and turned to a squaw that you would not back me against that lobo Mixler?"

"He had a little more backing than I could put out, did you notice?"

"Since when have we cared about the number of guns against us? I myself could outshoot any ten of them."

"You might outshoot any *one* of them — seeing Star Glynn wasn't there."

"You mean I am afraid of —"

"Take it cool, Josie. It was pretty rough. I wasn't sure what he was about until Daddy Bearsign started loading his wagon, and then it was too late. It wouldn't have made any difference, anyway. I couldn't have stopped Mixler, and neither could you, or the two of us together. He's the boss, and we've got to make the best of it all the way to the Belle Fourche."

José spat like one trying to take a bad taste out of his mouth. "*Sí.* So it is. I should not have called you a squaw." He pointed to the trampled fields. "But it was pretty rough trick. Some of those people lose everytheeng, just so we can save three days on the way to Montana. Maybe we will save no time at all, for there is rough country ahead, and we will have to turn westward anyway. And there had better be no more Willow Creeks."

"There won't be. Not from here. From here on she all belongs to Sitting Bull and his Sioux."

CHAPTER
NINE

The herd rolled on, through untouched grass already cured by the heat of summer. A dry rain rose in the west almost every afternoon with black clouds, thunder, and sometimes a cooling draught of moisture. They found water at Claus Coulee, at Henderson Creek, at the Niobrara.

Beyond Niobrara, Mixler turned the herd even farther eastward, thinking only of grass and water, ignoring the roughness of the country. It was hill and high prairie gashed by steep-sided coulees running down from the Black Hills, a teamster's hell.

As they pierced deeper into Indian country, Johnny Colt, Bill Spooner, and José were relieved of night-herd duty, spending their time on wide sweeps of the country, scouting for Sioux.

They would be gone for a day and night at a stretch, riding in the concealment of coulee bottoms, or sprawled for hours amid the rock and sage of some promontory, watching for war parties, returning to the herd only for fresh horses and food before setting out again.

The herd was now in a country untouched except by buffalo. To their right rose the purple, timbered summits of the Black Hills; dropping away to their left were the great plains of the upper Powder. Grass stood to the knees of their mounts; it blew in the wind; from the distance its wave patterns made it look like a buff-tan sea. And each day the signal smokes were visible, often so far no one could guess their distance, rising like vertical streaks of cloud to great height before bowing over and dissolving in the wind.

They camped at a spring on Yellowrobe Coulee and read the cold sign of a war party — the tracks of unshod horses, the blackened stick ends of a drenched fire, a pit lined with rawhide where antelope flesh had been cooked by means of red-hot stones. The rawhide had stiffened and turned brown around the top, pulling the stakes out, but its bottom was still filled with stones and grease scummed water. It was about two days old.

"Big war party?" Johnny Colt asked, trusting José's judgment on such things above his own.

"Feefteen."

"Sioux?"

He shrugged. "At home, I would say the Apache. But thanks to heaven the Apache are one thousand miles away."

They followed the trail for miles and lost it in grassland to the west. They camped, and drifted back through the quiet heat of morning and met Daddy Bearsign far ahead of the herd, jouncing along in the chuck wagon.

"Is there coffee water in that coulee?" Daddy asked.

Johnny said, "If you got a shovel. Green sign eight or nine miles over east."

"That's too damn far. I'll have to make it out of the scum bar'l. Been looking for Gonzales and Pecos, but I guess it's too early. They're scouting ahead for a camp site."

"They hadn't better scout too far. Saw where a Sioux party camped. They'll be looking for strays."

"I wouldn't worry about Gonzales. He's half Injun himself. All Mexicans are." He glanced at José. "Beg pardon, Josie. I didn't mean anything again you."

Johnny asked, "How's Mis' McCrae?"

"She's in miser'ble shape, Johnny. This is no place for a woman. Any man that'd load his woman in a wagon and follow a trail herd ought to be put through the Injun treatment. Why, that old Pittsburgh wagon of Jason's had to be water-soaked all night in the Red or he'd never even got her out of Texas, and McCrae's was even worse." He chawed tobacco, spat over the rumps of his team, and looked squinty-eyed to the west, where the country flattened out. "O' course, this rock-and-coulee route is probably more'n they expected."

"Agrees with the livestock," Big Bill said.

"They've even put on some tallow. By grab, maybe most of the humans will be dead when we raise Yellowstone, but the beef will be in fine shape."

Curly Phelps rode up in time to overhear Daddy. He said, "Yeah, but those hoeman won't thank Mix for anything. All those two-bit shanty outfits want is to get their busted-down wagons through."

At night there was a powwow at the upper camp. Mixler knew about it and stood around in the door of his wagon, looking that way.

94

"He's ready for 'em," Johnny Colt said, sprawled back in the shadow. "Four bits none of 'em will come."

José said, "He is killing that woman. In Chihuahua such a thing would never be allowed. In Chihuahua someone would have shot him already."

No one came. It was two nights and three rough coulee crossings later before a delegation from the other camp finally made an appearance. There were six men, headed by Rio Reavley.

Reavley rode closer than the others, and got down in the light of the fire. He looked very gaunt. His jaw had a long jut to it. He saw Mixler seated on a wagon tongue with a cup of coffee in his fingers, and walked that way on gangling, spavined legs.

"Hello, Rio," Mixler said, his voice unexpectedly casual. "Just in time for coffee."

"Thanks." Reavley didn't make a move toward the pot. He was scared of Mixler, like most of the others, and it had taken guts to walk up and face him. Now, to keep from showing his fear, he spoke in an aggressive voice. "What in hell are you trying to do, Mix — put us all afoot?"

Mixler took time to finish his coffee. He made a wry face at the dregs and tossed them away. He stood up. He looked beyond Reavley at the others — at Jason, at McCrae, and at gray-whiskered Wolf Carson.

"No, I'm not trying to put you afoot. And I'm not worrying about putting you afoot, either. That's *your* worry. Those cattle are what I'm worried about."

"The cattle are fine."

There was a slight hardening of Mixler's voice. "And they'll stay that way. Your cattle, and McCrae's cattle — everybody's cattle. They'll get to Montana with enough tallow to get 'em through one of those tough northern winters. Best route, best grass, most water. You follow any way you can. If those chicken-crate wagons of yours give out, try walking or crawling on your bellies. We've gone over all this before."

"I wish you'd come down to the wagon and tell that to McCrae's wife."

He laughed.

"I really mean it. I think if you'd see her —"

"Nobody asked him to bring her. And nobody asked Jason to bring his woman, or those whelps."

Wolf Carson, an easy-talking, likable old man, said, "Hell, Mix, there's a quicker way over west by the head-waters of the Powder. Give, us more time in Montana before blizzard."

Mixler didn't bother to answer.

McCrae, a beat-out little man, said, "Is it too much to ask just where you're headed?"

"No, I'll tell you where. Right now we're headed for the upper Warbonnet. We'll cross it by the old fur-company trail."

"How about Windham Coulee?"

"We're crossing that by the fur trail, too."

"There's no crossing there for a wagon."

Mixler's voice had become deadly. "Now, who could have told you that?"

When McCrae hesitated, Wolf Carson said, "I did."

"Maybe you're the one that's behind all this dissension, Wolf."

Reavley shouted, "No, he's not. I'm the one behind it, if you want to know. You've taken the tough road instead of the easy one ever since we left the Little Beaver. When Tom Mace objected —" He checked himself.

Mixler said, "Go on! Finish what you started to say!"

"All right, I will. You turned these gunmen o' yours loose on him, and they'd have killed him if he hadn't quit the herd. When Jason said something, you beat him half to death with your fists. Well, by the gawds, you ain't scared *me* out. I'll say what I think. It's this: You're trying to make it so almighty tough no wagon can follow you. You think because there's women and kids along, we'll have to shuck out. You think you can make us do it one after another and drive the whole shebang through to the Deergrass all by yourself, and when you get there you can pay us off trail price for abandoned beef!"

He was backing away as he talked. Mixler, rangy, with his bull neck and powerful shoulders sloped forward, followed him. Rage had turned Mixler's face an ashen color under his tan. His arms had thickened, tightening the denim material of his shirt. His hands, at the ends of long arms, were stretched down, the fingers extended.

Looking casual, Johnny Colt stood up. He moved away from the fire a trifle. His eyes swung to the shadows. He saw Andy Rasmussen, gangling, stooped, his hand on his Colt, budging it a trifle from its holster.

There were others, a man on each side — Star Glynn and Evas Williams. Reavley didn't realize they were there.

"Man behind you, Reavley!" he said softly.

His voice jarred the long, taut seconds of silence. Reavley had been ready to draw. He checked himself, spun, saw Rasmussen and the others. Very slowly Reavley moved his hands, lifting them wide of his body, away from his gun. He took a deep breath. Then he forced a bitter laugh and spoke to Mixler:

"Shoot me, Mix, and the time will come when every man in Montana Territory will know how it happened. That'll be a hell of a way to start in on a new range, won't it?"

Mixler in his fury temporarily lost control of his voice. He tried to speak and tried again. Then he turned away from Reavley and looked at Johnny Colt. This time he got words from his lips, through his teeth:

"You yellow turncoat!"

Vern Haltman got hold of his arm and swung him around. "Clay, use your head!"

He tore himself free. His strength sent the lighter man sprawling so he almost fell in the fire. Once more he turned on Reavley. "You or no other man is calling me a bushwhacker, or calling me a thief."

"Clay!" Vern Haltman shouted. "Both of you lost your tempers. Now get hold of yourself."

Mixler didn't turn, but the words registered. He said, "All right, Rio, if you and your friends don't like the way I'm running the outfit, you can get out."

"That suits us. We'll get started cutting our stock in the morning."

"No, you won't. You'll not cut a steer. If you go, you'll leave your cattle behind. I'm not delaying this herd a day or an hour."

Rio Reavley perked his lean shoulders in what was intended to be a laugh, but was actually nothing but an exhalation through his twisted lips. "So that's how it is!"

"Yes, that's how it is."

Reavley walked back to his horse and remounted. He nodded to the men who'd come with him, and led them out of sight in the early darkness.

Everyone was silent. Then Johnny Colt casually walked over, picked up his cup of coffee, drained it. He looked in the cup, tossed away the grounds. It was so quiet the pop of a burning stick in the fire jarred like gunshot.

Mixler watched him. He hitched his pants up, a characteristic movement that showed the stud-horse power of his legs.

Johnny said in his quiet drawl, "I think you mentioned 'yellow turncoat.' A man uses words like that when he's overwrought. Now you had time to think it over. You still want to call me them things, Mix?"

"What if I did?"

"Why, you're from Texas, like me. You know the answer to that."

"You got quite a reputation, haven't you?" Then Mixler decided to shrug it off. "I'd kill you, Johnny. As

I'm standing here, I'd kill you. But I'm not going to. I need you. I need you worse alive than dead."

Mixler and the Haltmans left. A strained silence fell over the camp. Men of the first watch kept riding in, pouring coffee, standing to drink it, always listening, watching. It was plain they expected trouble. Johnny Colt rolled up in his blankets. He slept and awoke suddenly with Big Bill over him, a hand on his shoulder.

He sat, and started pulling on his boots. "What's wrong?"

"They started cutting cattle."

"Who?"

"Reavley, Jason, and that bunch, o' course."

"Oh, sure. Where's Mixler?"

"I don't know. That's what worries me."

José was awake, too. He said, "Eh, Johnny, then it has come, the shoot-out, and I say *bueno*. At last we can settle the theeng one way or the other."

"We're still a long drift south of Deadwood in Injun country."

"Ha!"

"It's not funny, Josie. We've had no trouble from the Sioux because we're big. Wait until we're small. They'll whack us to pieces and be eating jerked beef for the next twelve months."

There was no one at Mixler's wagon, or at the Haltmans'. Some of the cowboys were snoring, and some, sensing trouble, were up, watching and listening.

They went to the rope corral. The wrangler was mounted and standing in the stirrups, looking far off toward the other camp. The herd was up, bawling and drifting.

"Oh, hello," he said.

"Where's Mix?"

"I don't know."

"He got his horse, didn't he?"

"Yeah, he took the big gray."

"How long ago was that?"

"I don't know. I roped so damned many horses tonight."

"*How long?*"

The tone of Johnny's voice scared him and he said, "I guess an hour and a half."

"Glynn, Rasmussen, Billy, that bunch, they were here, too, weren't they?"

"Yeah."

"What did they have in mind?"

"I don't know."

"You listened to their talk. You should know!"

"No, I don't! I didn't pay any attention."

"Which way did they ride?"

"I didn't pay any attention to that, either!" He raised his voice defensively. "Don't start any of your rough stuff with me! Damn it all, I'm only the horse wrangler here. I just work all night and all day for my ten a month and found. I ain't paid to mix up in any ruckus."

"Sure, kid. That's what I figured. And I'm not getting rough with you. Rope me the bay — that little bald-faced one. Wait, there's three of us and we're in a hurry. You run 'em by and we'll catch 'em."

The stars were commencing to fade and gray dawn to silhouette the foothill country to the east. The herd was up, drifting northward. A breeze carried the familiar smell of dust hide, hair, and manure — the odors of the trail herd.

Daddy Bearsign was awake and looking from the front drawstring of his wagon. His voice followed them as they rode at a swift trot over the bulge of ground from the rope corral: "What in the dirty, dyin' hell's going on? We driving beef by night and by day both? Ain't nobody staying for grub pile?"

They crossed ground that had been freshly trampled by the herd. Dawn was coming slowly, washing out the shadows that hung close to the earth, and, reining in atop a little rock-knobbed promontory, they had a view of the country.

Reavley and his men had been working long enough to get 150 head or so cut from the herd. Their wagons were up and moving. Two riders held the cut together, and kept it drifting. Other riders were busy herding small bunches of cattle over.

José moved with a sudden jerk and pointed toward the rim of a coulee about five hundred yards to the west. He said, "See? Five, seex men. You see the flash of that silver? That is the *concha* that Star Glynn wears on his hat. Now the trouble will start."

The six men made a tight group at a stiff gallop. They rode directly into the small herd and set it to milling.

One of the two cowboys guarding the herd stayed back, the other rode that way. He pulled up abruptly and tried to turn his horse. A gun exploded with a flash of powder visible in the early dawn light. Star Glynn or one of the others had drawn and fired.

The slug hit either the man or his horse. It was impossible to tell with the horse rearing and the man being dumped to the ground. The horse half slipped, got to his feet, and seemed to run directly over the fallen rider, but a second later they saw him clinging to stirrup and cantle, being half dragged, half carried from the place. He was jarred loose. He crawled to cover in the sagebrush with bullets kicking geysers of dirt over him.

José cried. "That was bushwhack! You theenk I will sit while —"

"Wait!"

Johnny Colt grabbed José's bridle and fought the horse around in a lunging cricle. Reavley, hearing the fight, was headed toward it at a gallop. Three men who had been working cattle followed him.

José cried, "Unhand my horse, señor! Do you think me an old squaw that I —"

"You'll wait till we see what's going on."

José cursed him in Spanish, English, and Apache, but he stopped trying to get the bridle free.

Reavley, after approaching to within 150 yards of Star's crew, suddenly reined to a stop. He bent over to drag his rifle from the scabbard. Bullets sent him in a headlong dive from his horse. He scrambled across the ground and out of sight in deep sage. There he started working his rifle with an accuracy that made Glynn and his men also abandon horse for the safety of the ground.

It had all consumed little more than ten seconds.

Johnny Colt, speaking through his teeth while still holding José's horse, said, "I can see, seh, you have never had army experience. In the army you never advance without determining the position of the enemy. See that dry wash? We'll head for it, then we'll ride up yonder, where that sage grows thick. We can raise plenty of hell with Star Glynn and his boys from there."

"Then let us ride!"

They spurred down the gentle slope. The dry wash was a wandering watercouse no more than twelve feet deep. It was necessary to place themselves no more than a hundred yards from Glynn's men in reaching it.

Over the rumble of galloping hoofs, Evas Williams' high-pitched voice could be heard: "No, it isn't — it's Johnny, the big fellow, and that damn Mexican!"

A bullet cuffed the air by Johnny Colt's cheek. A second came low, dug the earth with a glancing whine, and stung the forelegs of the bay with pellets of dirt and stone.

The horse made a sudden turn. The uneven ground made him lose footing. He fell to his side and nearly pinned Johnny's leg. Johnny extricated himself and dived clear, arms outstretched, his face in the dirt. The horse was pawing to get up. Johnny made a wild grab and retrieved the bridle. He got to his feet, spitting dirt. His six-shooter had fallen free. He limped after it, pulling the lunging horse.

He remounted. He was uncertain of directions. He rode, barely conscious of lead that scorched the air. The edge of the dry wash opened ahead of him. Next moment he was at the bottom, still in the saddle, with clouds of choking yellow-white dirt showering down.

"José?" he said. "Bill?"

"Here!" José called.

Bill said, "Bend over. This isn't very deep. Bend over before you get your head shot off."

He was talking to José. José said, "Bend over be damned! Thees is the day I will put an end to that bushwhack Star."

Johnny Colt regained his bearings. "Wait. Let's have a look."

José said, "I have waited too long already. Now is my time to shoot."

"Mixler isn't with that bunch."

"So we will get him later."

"Hold my horse."

He thrust the reins in José's hands and climbed crumbly dirt. He grabbed sage stalks and pulled himself over the edge. Sage hid his view. He went belly down through clumps of sage, until he found an opening where he could see more acres of sage with gunsmoke rising above it.

One of the wagons — it was Jason's — had turned around and the horses were running. Another, McCrae's, had turned enough to cramp the front wheels, and there one of the horses had gone down.

The horse was dead, with his weight pushing the wagon tongue into the ground. McCrae had crawled down from his seat and was trying to cut the straps, but it was impossible with the other horse lunging and kicking.

Suddenly McCrae stopped and dived back inside the wagon. A bullet had struck the wood beside him, leaving a white scar.

Johnny drew his six-shooter and fired twice into the sage where gunsmoke had puffed up, but it was a blind chance, a hundred-to-one chance, and bullets just as wild flew back at him.

He moved to a new place. It brought a new area under his vision. Far out, at the edge of the coulee, he glimpsed gun shine backed by the movement of men. They were only briefly in view. That would be Mixler and more of his men.

He slid back, crabwise, groping with his boots, avoiding cactus, punching the spent cartridge cases from his gun and reloading. He reached the edge of the dry wash and slid back to the bottom.

He said, "More men in that deep coulee, the one Star and his boys rode out of. See why Star was willing to get pinned down? Decoys. They're waiting for Reavley's help to come."

"For us, perhaps?"

"Us, Jason, Carson, everybody. This dry wash feeds into the coulee. We'll ride around, talk to 'em from behind."

At a gallop they followed the narrow, twisting gully. It deepened by unexpected steps. The walls became cut banks, and sage growing along the edges reached out to tear at their heads and shoulders. There was a sharp turn to the west, and the bottom fanned out to join the coulee.

They doubled back. Mixler, the three Haltman boys, and Andy Rasmussen were up the coulee side, against an undercut shale bank, as high as they could go without exposing themselves to the gun fight.

They heard the clatter of hoofs over stones in the bottom and turned with rifles ready.

"Call 'em off!" Johnny Colt called as he climbed rocky ground toward them.

Mixler said something from the side of his mouth to Rasmussen. He was long-jawed and narrow-eyed. He pulled his horse around, and the animal slid a few feet through loose dirt and stones. He clutched his Winchester in one hand with the barrel across the pommel. It covered Johnny Colt, and for a second all he needed to do was pull the trigger, but he resisted the temptation.

He waited for Johnny to come and said, "Now you're telling me what to do!"

"You trying to kill those women and kids?"

"We're killing no women and kids."

"Look at McCrae's wagon — one horse down and them chopping it to pieces with Winchesters."

Mixler climbed his horse, looked over the edge, and laughed. "Oh, hell, they'll be all right." He rode back. "Nothing short of a buffalo Sharps would go through an oak wagon box at that range."

"You're not calling 'em off?"

Mixler shouted, "No!" His lips were pulled tight, showing his powerful, clenched teeth. "No, I'm not! Let 'em get to hell away with their rigs the same way they got in. I'm letting nobody cut my herd until I give the word."

"Mix!" Vern Haltman cried. He motioned his brothers away with one hand and guided his horse down the slope with the other, jostling Mixler's horse in the process and getting between him and Johnny Colt just as it looked like a shoot-out.

Mixler tried to ride clear. "Get out of my way!"

"Mix, this'll do no good."

"It'll do me some good. I've taken all —"

"I'm one of the owners here, don't forget that." Mixler stared at him as though the blood in his head had blinded him. Vern said, "We could all stretch rope for a thing like this if word gets to Montana. They'll do it if we kill any woman or child."

"They rode into it," Mixler growled, but Vern's remark about a rope had set him to thinking, and a pursed look of worry appeared around his mouth. He rode back to the brow of the coulee and bellowed, "Hold it, yonder! Hold it! I told you to stay clear of those wagons."

The shooting tapered off. Mixler had ridden twenty or thirty yards in the open when a bullet made him turn back. He found cover in the coulee and looked at Johnny. "All right," he said, "I stopped *my* boys, let's see you stop yours."

"They're not my boys, seh. They're all yours, if you were man enough to accept responsibilities."

"Brother's keeper!" He laughed with a hard backward jerk of his head. "You sound like a preacher."

108

"That, seh, is not an insult."

Johnny Colt borrowed José's white kerchief, tied it to the barrel of his Winchester, and rode into the open.

He heard Reavley's voice: "Put that gun down, Pancake!"

Pancake Charley was Reavley's cook. Men from both sides started moving into view. Reavley and his men were scattered in the concealment of grass clumps and sage wherever a depression in the earth gave them protection against bullets.

Reavley, gangling and limping, came forward, a six-shooter in one hand, his rifle in the other.

"He'll call it quits if you do," Johnny said.

"What do you mean, quits?"

"He's boss of the outfit."

Reavley got hold of Johnny's saddle leather, took a deep breath, shook his head, and let a bitter laugh through his lips. "The boss? Say, he sure as hell means to be!"

"That's right, Rio. He has the guns to back him up, too."

Rio rested and thought. He kept hold of the saddle and watched Star Glynn, who was walking toward Mixler. He called Glynn a bitter name. "Did you see him try to gun down Al Geppert?"

"Was that Gepp? I think he was only winged."

"Not Star's fault. I didn't think he'd go that far — Mix, I mean. Didn't think he'd cut loose. Figured he'd let us cut our stock when the showdown came. Proves that the old poet was right — 'Never play aces in another man's game.' Now what'll he do? — take our stock and run us out?"

"No, he's too worried about trouble when he gets to Montana. More law in Montana than here. Those gold camps have things organized. Might find a Helena sheriff waiting for him on the other side of the Yellowstone."

"Well, that Helena sheriff had better have some deputies if he goes to take that Mixler."

CHAPTER
TEN

There was a wounded man on each side — Al Geppert with a flesh wound high on his right arm, and one of Haltman's punchers, who had narrowly escaped death when the breech of his rifle blew out, cutting his right cheek and tearing a chunk from his ear.

The dead horse was cut from the traces of McCrae's wagon, another was hitched in. The herd moved on. Callie McCrae, lying in her bed on the wagon floor, moaned and wept alternately, and Mrs. Jason, kneeling over her, kept rubbing her hands and soothing her with reassurances.

"There, there! It was just a few stray hits on the wagon box, Callie. They weren't trying to kill *you.* Everything will be all right now."

No one had breakfast. The herd was moving too fast. There was a cold wagon lunch at noon. Camp for the night was made a little earlier than usual along some sinkhole water where two coulees joined at a place called Sloughwater Flats.

Men washed off their dirt and sweat in stale warm water that soon was hoof-trampled to mud. They ate beef, beans, and dumplings, gulping them down like winter wolves, and drank muddy coffee made of the muddy water.

They finished and lay around the sagebrush fire. There was little of the rough joking of former nights. Although most of them were working cowboys, not directly involved in the fight, few of them shed their guns in their bedrolls. Mixler remained in his wagon, and the Haltmans around theirs. Star Glynn and his men ate by themselves, a close group, heads together, speaking quietly, sometimes bursting forth in private heehaws that seemed a little forced.

Lying by Daddy's wagon, Johnny Colt said, "They're building up to something. They didn't look much like gunmen in that fight this morning, and it troubles 'em. They got the idea everybody's laughing behind their backs, and for a gunman there's nothing much worse."

José said, "And who will be their target? You, us. See how they tried to keel us this morning."

"Yep, that's how it is."

"You are very calm about thees thing, señor."

"When I step on a rattlesnake I'm not surprised when he strikes at me."

Big Bill muttered, "Well, when I see a snake coiled up in the sagebrush I don't generally stick my bare toe out at him, and that's what we're doing when we stay in this camp. They sure *do* have something in their craws."

Johnny laughed and yawned and looked at the sky. It was very clear now, with night long settled and the dust cleared away.

"You know what happened to Tom Mace," Bill said.

"Not exactly. Anyhow, I'm not Tom Mace. I got a couple of good friends that Tom didn't have."

José nudged him with his boot toe, and Johnny, without turning, saw that Rasmussen had slouched over to the fire. He bent and swished the coffee around in the pot to see if a cupful remained. Several cups remained, but he didn't want coffee. He put the pot back and said to Johnny:

"You said something last night, and the more I think about it, the less I like it."

Johnny rolled over to a half-sitting position. He rested on his left elbow, his right hand free. With a spear of buffalo grass he picked his teeth and waited.

Rasmussen said, "What'd you have on your mind when you told Rio Reavley there was a man behind him? Did you mean I'd shoot him in the back?"

"I heard someplace," Johnny said softly, spitting out fragments of grass, "that you'd killed a man or two from the blind side. Tell you where they told me that — It was down at Fort Addison. Of course, I wouldn't know. I never saw you in action."

Rasmussen's purpose had been to swagger a little and show everyone there that he wasn't a damned bit afraid of Johnny Colt, no matter what had happened that morning. Now it had gone further than he had intended. The Fort Addison thing had been brought up, and all the boys were watching to see what his response would be.

He decided to have a cup of coffee after all. He placed a cup on the ground and poured. After filling the cup, he put it down with his right hand and leaned

113

for the cup with his left. In lifting the cup, he spilled some of the coffee. It was deliberate, intended to distract attention from one hand to the other. He said, "Ouch!" and reached with his right hand for the six-shooter on his thigh.

It was a good trick, but not good enough. He had telegraphed it with his eyes. Johnny Colt drew without standing, with an upward sweep of his hand, a stiffening of his body. He hesitated a fragment of time, a hesitation that recognized the fact that the first draw meant nothing without the accuracy to back it up. Then his gun came to life with a clap of explosion lashing flame and lead across the fire.

He had resisted the temptation to kill Rasmussen. Instead, he aimed at his wrist. With ten steps separating them, with Rasmussen strongly revealed by the fire, it was an easy shot.

The slug struck Rasmussen's forearm. The force of it turned him halfway around. He was still up, reeling and glassy-eyed. He fell to his knees, grabbed his bullet-ripped arm, and stared at it as blood ran in swift streams from the tips of his fingers.

For a shocked second, nobody moved. Johnny got up. He stood with his gun drawn, the barrel elevated a trifle, a wisp of powder smoke trailing from it.

"I'm not looking for trouble," he said in a clear voice. "All I want is to get to Deadwood with nine hundred steers. Maybe I'll do it, too. Me and my friends. If you had any idea of getting rid of me the way you got rid of Tom Mace, you better send somebody better'n Andy around to do it. And I'll give you warning right now.

114

Next one, if I'm lucky enough to outdraw him, is going to need more'n a bone-setter. He's going to need a man with a shovel."

He laughed when he finished. He didn't look at anyone in particular, though he didn't lose trace of Star Glynn.

Mixler had been inside the Haltman wagon. He came out and shouted, "Who fired that shot?"

Johnny said, "Andy and me, we just came to an understanding."

"You want to start those cattle to running?"

"A man doesn't consider those things when his life is on the line."

Mixler swung around, addressing the camp in general. "If you want to kill each other, that's your own business. But if anybody stampedes that herd, I'll drag him to death on forty feet of lariat behind a horse. And that's a promise. That's a solemn promise I intend to keep."

Next day two men arrived from the south. They were Ed Ward and Kiowa Jim.

Big Bill said, "You don't suppose they killed that poor old man?"

"Tom Mace? Don't worry too much about that poor old man."

José said, "One at a time they will try to kill us. In the dark, in the back. They are afraid of you now that you outdrew Rasmussen. We had better steek together, the three of us, and maybe carry two guns instead of one, or we will not be three happy men riding to Deadwood. We will be three dead men riding nowhere."

That night at grub pile Johnny Colt hunkered behind Ed Ward with his tin plate and coffee, well knowing that his presence made the gunman nervous.

"I seem to recollect your face from Maverly, seh. You stayed around town after we left?"

"What of it?"

"Now, seh, you're nervous. Nothing about my question should make you nervous. Look, you've spilled your coffee, and coffee is hard to come by on the trail."

Ward steadied the cup. His eyes darted over to Kiowa Jim. Jim was trying to hear, but he was too far away, so he got up and lounged that way.

Johnny went on very casually, "Somebody tried to bushwhack us in those wagon freight yards, only they were scared to get close enough. Y'know, some men are too yellow-gutted even to make good bushwackers."

Ed Ward was so tense and trembly he gave up on the coffee and put it down. "Why you telling me all this? If you think —"

"I don't know who did it. That's the truth, I really don't. But you stayed on, and I sort of wondered if the law there in —"

Kiowa said, "You got out alive." His lips smiled, but there was no smile in his dark Indian eyes. "What the hell? Lots of men take shots at me. I get out alive. I was lucky, you was lucky."

"I been lucky for a long time."

Ed Ward, feeling better with Kiowa backing him, said beneath a curled lip, "Ever think your luck might change?"

"Now, what would you mean by that?"

Ward straightened his skinny frame in a manner that made the six-shooter a trifle handier to his right hand, but the hand was still high, his thumb in movement, poking a piece of his shirttail in. He did not answer.

Johnny Colt went on with his old drawl, "Now, Ed, don't be a fool and go for that gun. That's not your style. Play it safe. Just like those boys in the wagon yard."

Later, in their blankets, José rolled over to ask, "What did you say to that Ed Ward?"

"I wanted to find out if it was him that tried to pot-shot us in Maverly."

"Ha! Of course it was heem."

"Well, I had to know."

He slept and awakened suddenly. It was quiet. The cook fire had burned down to a bed of coals. José and Big Bill snored. The wrangler was talking to somebody at the rope corral, but it hadn't been the wrangler that awakened him. Then he saw Lita Haltman and Mixler, large and small shadows, at the forward end of the Haltman wagon. They were standing close together. Her head was turned a little, and he realized that Mixler was saying something in a quiet voice.

He went hot and cold. He hated Mixler. He wanted to kill him.

He tried to laugh at himself. It was none of his business. The girl was a breed. Breeds were all alike.

They followed any man who crooked his finger. He didn't give a damn about her. He tried to tell himself these things, and lie back down to sleep. But he sat and watched with hatred gnawing through his abdomen.

They were silent for a long while, then he realized that she was trying to get away from him, and that he was holding her. He started to get up, stopped. He had imagined she was crying. She wasn't. She was laughing, fighting back the sound.

Suddenly she stopped. They parted quickly. Mixler walked off. She ran around the wagon, started up the steps, stopped. Vern Haltman, inside, said something.

She went in. There was no other sound. He still watched. Bright moonlight shone on the wagon top, and through it and he could see the hint of her shadow as, minutes later, she moved by her bed, bent and stood and bent again, undressing, fingering through her hair, rebraiding it.

He slept poorly and awoke with a burned taste in his mouth. He didn't give a damn if she sneaked away at night with Mixler. He kept telling himself that, but he still watched for her, and it gave him a jolt when he saw her far away, riding at a gallop, riding nowhere, just for the kid pleasure of feeling the wind in her face.

José came up beside him. José's eyes were shrewd and there was a smile on his lips as he fashioned and lighted a cigarette.

"Windham Coulee," he said, jerking his head northward. "We get there pretty quick. Or were you not looking at Windham Coulee?"

"What the hell did you think I was looking at?"

"Ha, Johnny! Don't tell a Spanish-Irish half-breed about women, or about men when they are thinking about women."

Windham Coulee was a deep gash, or network of gashes, from one to four miles in width, sundering the country that sloped down from the Black Hills. Here and there roads had been dug for the carts of fur traders traveling north from Fort Laramie, but that had been long ago, and erosion had almost obliterated them.

Johnny Colt, Bill, and José, riding back along the rim after scouting for Indians, found Daddy Bearsign with his wagon at the jumping-off place where one of the roads could still be seen zigzagging along benches and dirt banks to the bottom.

"How's it look?" Bill asked.

"Look for yourself." Daddy sat with his legs over the side of the spring seat and aimed a spurt of tobacco juice at the cut-bank rim. "How'd you like the job of taking this center-sprung hooligan wagon down a goat trail like that?"

Bill said, "Wait till Mixler sees it. This time he'll have to back up."

"Maybe," Johnny said.

"Well, look at it!"

"I'd never bet on Mixler backing up. He'd run this outfit over the black rim of hell before backing up."

Several more wagons had rolled into sight over a hump of the prairie. The first to come up was Reavley's, with Fred Jardine driving.

Jardine took a long, squinty look at the depths and said, "How's he going to navigate *that?*"

"He ain't!" Bill said, still chuckling.

Ellis Haltman, in Tom Mace's low-wheeled supply wagon, reached the coulee half a mile farther along, where Gonzales and Whitey Fischer were exploring along the sides. Ellis stood in the seat and signaled with his hat.

Daddy Bearsign said, "I'll wager they found some way of makin' it even tougher."

He drove over with the team at a trot and the cook wagon at a careening gallop behind them. Pots, pans, and the tin dishes in the plunder box made a rattle that could be heard for a mile. Gonzales rode out fifty yards to meet him. He showed his teeth in a grin and said something, gesturing at the coulee.

"What?" Daddy asked, getting the wagon to a stop.

"See? A new road. I should be Jeem Bridger the trail blazer."

"You should be hung by your own dewlap."

"Well, maybe ees not pavement like Denver City, but what do you expect out on the cattle trail?"

Jardine shook his head. "We might make it, but McCrae never will. That old wagon of his is just loose boards tied together with rawhide, and that old Pittsburgh of Jason's isn't much better. You know how old that Pittsburgh is? Why, the army brought it in during the Mexican War."

Ellis Haltman and Gonzales went down on foot to explore a road while the others waited. They were still out of sight when McCrae and Jason rolled up.

McCrae, without saying anything, sat hunched and dejected in the seat, looking into the coulee depths.

Johnny rode up beside him and said, "Hello, Mac. How's your missus?"

McCrae shook his head. "Oh, tol'able," he said, in a manner that showed she wasn't tol'able at all. "She's sick with what her sister had. The gallstones. She had some rest earlier when we crossed those flat gumbo sinks, but this bunch grass is like a washboard. It pains her to get jounced around." He nodded toward the depths of the Windham. "She'll sure as hell get jounced down there."

"If I was you, I'd drive that woman back to Cheyenne," Daddy said. "They got a doc there, a Chinyman, and he treats them bowel stones with some sort of dried leaf he gets all the way from Frisco. I had a pal one time, he was camp cook when U-P was building, and he had the bowel stones so bad he was doubled with his knees higher than his ears and even whisky wouldn't help him. Well, we hauled him in on the work train and the Chink went to work on him, filling him with that green herb and gallons of soapy water. Pretty soon it put him to sleep with every muscle limp as a baby, and two days later he shucked them stones, a handful of 'em like the marbles you use playin' Kelly pool, and he ain't had an attack since."

The thin face of Callie McCrae appeared in the opening of the Conestoga. She was probably no more than thirty-five, but she looked fifty. She was pale from her weeks under the wagon top, thin, with stringy hair. Seeing her, Daddy Bearsign took off his dusty hat.

121

She said, "Who was this doctor?"

"Called himself Hung Gow, or something that sounds like that."

"Is he there now? Do you know if he still treats folks?"

McCrae said, "We can't go back there. You heard where he was, didn't you? All the way back in Cheyenne."

She was ready to cry. "Why can't we, Gayle? It's just as close as Montana. Why can't we turn around and go back to Cheyenne? We'll find other range thereabouts."

"Because the wagon would never hold up. It wouldn't get us back to the Platte."

She pointed at the coulee. "How long will it last down there?"

He said doggedly, "We'll get through somehow if we stay with the herd. If our wagon gives out, we'll travel with Reavley. I'll get you to Miles. There'll be a doctor in Miles. Maybe a Chink doctor, if that's what you need."

The herd, now on the graze, had topped a hump of the prairie a couple of miles away. Four riders came in sight and cut across toward the supply wagon. One of them was Mixler, another was Lita Haltman.

The woman retreated to her bed, where the sobbing wail of her voice could be heard: "Gayle, you know what he's trying to do. He's trying to wreck our wagons and kill us all. I told you at Brazos how it'd be. Them big outfits like Mixler and the Haltmans never had any interest in poor folks except to kill 'em off for their own profit."

Lita Haltman had ridden up in time to hear. She stood in the stirrups and cried, "That's not true!"

"It's true, and you know it's true!"

"Callie!" McCrae said. "Look at all the nights Lita's come around and set up with you."

She kept wailing, "White trash, that's what we are to them. We're not God's creatures, just white trash."

After running out of words, she kept crying. It made Johnny feel sick and sweaty. He wanted to help her, but there was nothing he could do. Just nothing. This was Indian country. They couldn't turn back. They had to go on, across Windham, across other coulees as bad. If the wagon fell apart, they would have to double up. If all the wagons fell apart, they'd have to ride, or walk, or crawl, or die.

After that first moment, Lita got over her anger. Her dark quarter-blood eyes were on Johnny Colt. She said, "You're still figuring to split off and drive to Deadwood?"

"That's my idea."

"There are doctors in Deadwood. Couldn't you get her there?"

"I don't know. Maybe there's tracks for a wagon and maybe not. We'll have to wait and see."

Mixler was obviously curious about their reaction to Windham Coulee. There was a very slight smile at the corners of his lips. He had been waiting for the moment, and now he enjoyed it.

Johnny Colt turned away, calling him a name under his breath. "A man ought to shoot him."

José nodded. "*Si*. We will tell him that this is the end, here, this edge of the deep coulee, and if he does not like it, poof! One from the Colt forty-five, eh?"

"He's still the boss. All the way to Belle Fourche."

"You are sure it will end there, at the Belle Fourche?"

"We'll see."

"You are singing in the dark, and your song is the song of a fool. Each day it is coming, a little closer, the day you will kill that man, or he will kill you."

Mixler had ridden to McCrae's wagon. He tried to look inside. "Got your wife in there?"

"Yeah."

"Better move her. Carry her down. That rig of yours is likely to fall apart on one of the steep pitches."

She had stopped sobbing to listen. She wailed, "No, I'm not budging an inch. I'm staying right here in my own bed."

"They can move your bed."

"I won't!" She sounded hysterical. It sounded like overwrought laughter. "I'm staying right here in this wagon. You can't make me leave this wagon."

"Suit yourself!" He said to McCrae, "But if she gets spilled down a cut bank, don't blame us."

McCrae tried to reason with his wife, but she wouldn't listen. Her hysteria mounted. Dave Jason's wife came running, holding her skirts to keep them from catching on the sage, and climbed in over the end gate.

124

Johnny could hear her saying, "Now, Callie, you got to listen to me. You got to move your bed like he said. It'll only be to the bottom."

Mixler laughed with a heavy jerk of his shoulders. Without waiting for the result of Mrs. Jason's pleading, he shouted, "All right, Tommy. You go down first. See if you can get that outfit to the first ledge. Then stop there. We'll have to lock the hind wheels on the next pitch. Take it slow with the brake set, then bring it around sharp as you can."

The wagon was built low to the ground, with wide, solid wheels that made it a rough rider across the bunch grass of the prairie, but added to its durability, giving it a low-slung center of gravity. It took the first pitch; then, with hind wheels snubbed by a hickory pole, it was skidded down a steep bank of clay with dust billowing over it. From there, checked only by the hand brake, it was guided down a twisting, turning switchback from one rock reef level to another to the final cut-bank descent. After some wrangling between Tommy and Ellis Haltman, the team was unhitched, a post was set in a rock crevice, and the wagon was lowered, tail gate first, by means of doubled lariat drops. The descent had taken half an hour, and the first steers were along the crests, bawling, sniffing the air for the smell of water.

"Get them wagons started down!" Mixler bellowed. "Get 'em started before that herd tramps out what road we got."

The cook wagon was next. More ungainly and top-heavy, it clung precariously to the switchback, but it reached the bottom without incident. Then came Mixler's wagon, and Haltman's and Reavley's and Jason's.

The brakes on Jason's wagon had recently been repaired with rawhide shoes. Pressure of the descent made one of the brake shoes loosen. The wagon continued with one wheel locked, the opposite one rolling free. To stop his momentum, Jason had to swing sharply into a bank. The wagon came to a stop in precarious balance. An unnatural strain falling on the left front wheel cracked two of the spokes.

"Keep going!" Mixler bellowed. "You can't stop there and fix your rig. Bring it on to the bottom."

Jason got his team turned. The injured wheel held as it rolled along the slanting surface of the bench. The hand brake was useless. He got down the next pitch by whipping his horses, turning them hard, keeping them away from the plummeting wagon.

Big Bill ran beside the wagon, shouting, "Pull up! Pull up, you fool! You'll have to get the hind wheels snubbed."

Jason tried, but it was too late. The wagon was too heavily loaded, rolling too fast. The team, frightened by the wagon, plunged and ran. The wagon careened on its wobbly wheel. The wheel flopped back and forth with loose spokes banging against the underframe. The reef petered out. It slanted more and more steeply. He pulled the team around, downhill, and thus saved the wagon for an instant. He might even have reached safety, but the strain of turning was too much for the crippled wheel. It collapsed altogether. The wagon

126

dived forward, crashed one corner of the box with a shower of soft clay, and rolled on its side.

A projection of shale held it for a moment. Jason had fallen to earth, face down, the reins still in his hands. He got to his feet. Supplies showered over him. A barrel of flour broke. Somehow he managed to climb between the team and wagon without being kicked to death, and reached the uphill side. A second later the wagon slipped off the shale projection. It slowly rolled over, dragging the horses with it. The horses, tangled in harness, would have kicked each other to death, but Gonzales, wiry and quick as a weasel, sprang in with his clasp knife and cut the tugs.

The wagon rolled again and again, gathering momentum. It came back on its wheels. It raced in a quarter circle, hurtled the final forty feet, and ended upside down, a demolished mass of warped boards, timbers, and rawhide.

"By grab," Daddy Bearsign said, "there's wood for supper and we won't even have to chop it."

For a moment nobody knew whether Jason's wife and kids were inside. Vern Haltman ripped the canvas away, looking for them. Then he saw the woman atop the coulee rim, eyes shaded by her forearm. The younger boy, behind her, was holding to her skirts and bawling.

"Shut up!" she shouted. "Shut up that howlin'. Ain't it enough we saved Paw and the horses?"

Somehow it sounded funny. Even Jason stood and wiped flour out of his eyes and laughed. "Damn, yes.

Paw and the horses. They sure got me lumped in the right company."

McCrae waited in his wagon at the brink of the coulee. His face looked haggard, grayish under its tan. He watched the laughing men with the dull manner of one who fails to comprehend. His wife was still in her bed. She felt the sudden slant of the wagon and called out to him.

Rio Reavley, standing in the coulee bottom, cupped his hands and shouted, "Hey, get her out of there. McCrae! McCrae!"

But McCrae kept on going. Gonzales, Big Bill, and a couple of Mixler's punchers were the only ones close enough to do anything, and of these only Big Bill and Gonzales started for the wagon.

Bill reached its rear, got a handhold on the end gate, and boosted himself so he could look inside. Dust rolled through the cracks of the bottom. The woman lay on her back on an old hair mattress, arms wrapped over her face.

"Stop the rig!" he bellowed at McCrae, and when that did no good he turned to Gonzales, who by now was just above, running, his boots holding precariously in the clay back. "See if you can get hold of the team!"

He crawled inside. The wagon lurched and turned, almost knocking him off his feet. He got to one knee beside Callie McCrae. "Mis' McCrea. I'm getting you outside over the end gate."

She wailed, "Stay away! Go away and leave me alone! I don't care if I die. I'm not leaving this wagon."

128

The wagon came to a stop. Big Bill gathered her up, mattress and all, and carried her to the back just as Johnny Colt rode up.

Johnny dismounted, lowered the end gate, and helped get her outside. There Big Bill took over again, carrying her as easily as he would a child, talking to her as though she were a child, half sliding, half walking, all the way to the bottom.

Johnny Colt, following a different route, preceded him to the bottom. He got his own bed from the low-wheeled supply wagon and placed it on the ground for her, then he rode on to help hold back the cattle.

Men were carrying things downhill to lighten McCrae's wagon, and Callie, seeing them, sat up and started to wail again:

"That's all my good fancywork. Don't let 'em stack it on the ground."

Bill talked to her in his gentle voice. "There, now, Mis' McCrae. Don't you worry. It won't be left. We'll keep the cows from trompin' it."

The wagon was half filled with odds and ends of furniture, framed pictures, boxes of bric-a-brac, the cheap junk that the woman had come to treasure.

Star Glynn rode up, stopped, looked at it, laughed. "Holy hell! What we running, a church bazaar? No wonder the wagon broke down. Whyn't you dump it and leave it?"

Callie cried, "You tell him to keep away."

Bill said, "You heard her. Keep away from it."

"From that I'll keep a *long* way," Star said, and spurred off at a gallop.

Finally, lightened and with men helping, McCrae's wagon made the descent, but the strain sprung one of its front tires.

Big Bill called for McCrae to stop. "The wheel! Wait, maybe we could pull a good one off that wreck of Jason's."

"No. Bastard size. Have to mend it." He looked for wire. Cattle were piling up along the rim, bawling, and riders were holding them back.

Mixler rode back at a gallop. "Get agoing!" His voice was hoarse from shouting. "Get that woman inside. Get rolling. Two minutes and the herd will trap you. If it does, don't expect us to get you out. We'll leave you and to hell with you."

Bill tried to tell him about the wheel.

He brought his horse around with a hard twist and said, "I don't give a damn about the wheel."

"They can hold those cattle a while yet."

"Don't tell *me* what they can do!"

Big Bill was slow to anger, but a hatred of Mixler had long grown inside him. He stepped back from the wheel.

"Well, I *am* telling you! You gone far enough. You hold those cattle back!"

"Or what will you do?"

"You ain't got *me* buffaloed. You think you're one hell of a man, but I don't. You're just tough because you got men at your back."

Mixler sat for a few seconds with his hand opening and closing above his gun. Big Bill carried no gun. He had taken it off for the sake of lightness and cached it somewhere.

Mixler said, "You picked your time."

"What do you mean?"

"I mean that I'd kill you if you had a gun on."

"I'll get my gun if —"

"I'll fight any man on this drive any way he chooses. I'll fight him with guns, or I'll fight him like a wolf with the weapons I was born with."

He swung down and tied his bridle to the rear wheel. He did it all without taking his eyes off Big Bill. He walked forward with his arms down and his big fists doubled. When he got close he feinted with a short left, and walking straight on, came up with a right.

For a big man, Mixler was quick. Bill failed to stop the blow. It caught him on the jaw. It snapped his head to one side. His hat flew off. He was glassy-eyed for a second, but he recovered himself. He was still on his feet. He charged, swinging haymaker lefts and rights, carrying Mixler before him.

He tried to pin Mixler against the wagon, but Mixler fell backward to the ground. He did it deliberately. He lit on his back, his elbows braced behind him, and drove both feet upward to Bill's groin.

Mixler stood up and brushed dirt off his pants. Bill was on the ground, writhing, blind and breathless from pain. Mixler ignored him. He looked around. Eight or ten men had ridden up in time to see the short battle. There was satisfaction in his manner when he saw the size of his audience. He remounted and said in a voice that carried out above the bawling cattle:

"I understand there's been some argument about who's the best man in this outfit. I belong to the old school that believes a trail boss should be able to lick any man he's got under him." He swept his arm in a signal to let the cattle move forward. "Come on, get rolling. Let 'em come, boys! Let 'em ramble!"

Big Bill was still paralyzed from the blow. Using his hands, he reached the wagon and pulled himself up, but he was still not able to make his legs function.

McCrae said, "Get inside the wagon."

"In your wife's bed, I suppose. No, bring my horse."

He tried to vomit and couldn't. Blood ran from the corners of his mouth; there were bits of sage in his hair.

A cowboy led the horse around and Bill managed to get in the saddle. Johnny, riding back through the dust and bawling of cattle, helped McCrae carry his wife inside, helped load the last of his things and get the wagon to rolling.

"What happened to you?" he asked Bill, shouting to be heard.

"I run into one. I asked for it."

Cattle were on both sides, in front, and behind. McCrae swung his whip, urging the team. Every quarter mile he had to stop to kick the sprung tire back in place.

The bottoms broadened. There were groves of cottonwoods. A spring-fed stream flowed from one of the feeder gullies, but already it had been trampled to mud by the herd. The lead steers had stopped, and others were piling in on them. The wagons went on alone to another spring, flowing clear and cold from an undercut strata of sand rock.

Johnny found Big Bill helping McCrae with the wheel.

"Now tell me what happened. You fight with Mixler?"

"I was licked, that's all."

"Kicked in the groin!" McCrae said. "Call that being licked if you want to."

"When a man's licked, he's licked. Out on the trail they never ask how."

By working through the night, they repaired the wagon. It rolled on with the others along a coulee bottom that became a hell of rock and gullies. The iron tire, pulled into place by wrappings of heat-shrunken rawhide, worked loose again. One of the spokes cracked. It was repaired, and it gave out again, this time with a shock that took the other front wheel with it.

Everything slid to the forepart of the wagon. They unhitched the horses and got Callie outside. Her husband, dust-coated, sat staring at his smashed wagon. Shock seemed to glaze his senses.

"We'll have to leave it," Reavley said. "You hear me, Mac?"

He finally got up and helped them.

Reavley made room for Mrs. McCrae by throwing some of his supplies away. They went on, pressed by the herd.

Returning at night after a day of scouting for Indian sign, Johnny Colt called McCrae to one side and said, "Your wife can't take it any more, Mac. I think you'd better head for Fort Lodgepole. You'll have to use our wagon and that big team of grays. You can make it in forty-eight hours."

"How about my cows? There's only four hundred of 'em, but they're all I got in the world."

"We'll cut 'em out with ours and drive to Deadwood. If you're lucky, it'll make you a fortune."

"Mixler'll never let you do it. *You* ain't driving to Deadwood. Nobody is. That Rocking A stock will go all the way to Montana whether you like it, or Tom Mace likes it. Mixler won't let anybody split the herd."

On the following day, Reavley's wagon became a three-wheeled cripple. After a night of work, hacking spokes from green cottonwood, it rolled again, and gave out before the morning was half gone.

Jason said, "No use trying to repair it. Hold on. Haltman has an extra wheel."

"Does us no good," McCrae said. His voice showed him beaten, ready to quit, ready to lie down in the hot dirt and die.

"Vern isn't so bad." He called his boy Nubbins over. "You go ask for the wheel. It'll be harder to turn down a kid."

Vern was driving the big wagon. He stopped when Nubbins hailed him, and sat looking down into his face. The kid was skinny. His hair hadn't been cropped since Texas, and now hung over his shirt collar. He wore a Confederate Army hat so old it retained no semblance of its original shape. It rose to a point in the crown, the band had long ago disappeared, and the brim flopped down so he had to tilt his head back in order to see. His shirt and pants had been blue, but now they were rags bleached almost white. On his feet were some cast-off boots with the sides broken out. Somewhere he'd picked up an old belt and holster. The belt loops were filled with shot-out cartridge cases, the holster was empty.

Nubbins had plenty of fire and fight to him, and he showed it now, asking for help but not begging it, not getting down in front of a Haltman.

"They sent me," Nubbins said, meaning Reavley and his dad. "Said they couldn't roll an inch without another wheel. Said you were carrying an extra wheel forward in the cook wagon."

Vern hated to say no to him. "That's Mixler's wheel, not mine."

"He wouldn't give it to me, you know that."

"I'll see him about it."

"When?"

Vern stopped talking and looked back toward the herd. Mixler, mounted on a big-barreled gray, came at a gallop.

He stopped with a shower of dirt and addressed the boy roughly. "Now what have you come to beg for?"

Nubbins was scared of him and ready to bawl. "I ain't beggin'."

Mixler laughed. He took off his hat, wiped sweat on the heel of his hand, and laughed again. "Well, what do you want?"

Vern said, "Reavley sent him. He wants that extra wheel Daddy's carrying in the cook wagon."

Addressing Nubbins, Mixler asked, "What happens when the cook wagon breaks down?"

"I don't know."

"You don't know! Well, I do. When she breaks down, we'll have that extra wheel to keep it rolling. You go back there and tell Reavley and your dad that they'll have to rawhide their stuff together just like they have for the last thousand miles." Watching the kid ride off, he added, "I don't know how many times I have to tell 'em these things."

Vern, fighting an angry tremble, said, "They can't fix that wagon any more. They tried to build a new wheel out of cottonwood. You can't put a load on it."

"Have they tried lightening their load? Ever look inside that wagon? Filled with old picture frames and rocking chairs and family Bibles."

"They threw that stuff away. All they got now is Callie and her bed and some grub."

"Well, it's not our lookout. From here on they can drop out and the hell with them. They've been a stone around our necks ever since we crossed the Nations."

He'd have ridden away then, only Vern stopped him. "Clay!"

He reined up. "Yeah?"

"You know what they'll say about us up in Montana if we show up with those cattle and no owners. It looks like a poor way to start business in a new territory."

"Still worrying about that! You're a tenderhearted fellow, Vern. You always had plenty of mercy on everybody. So did your dad. That's why you were up to your tailbone in debt and needed me to get you out of

Texas. Now you'd like to do the same thing all over again, and you'll be welcome to once we're in Montana. But not here. Not here, Vern, my boy, because here it's being done my way."

CHAPTER
ELEVEN

Mixler merely shrugged when Johnny Colt rode to him and said that he had decided to give the McCraes and Jasons his flat-wheeled supply wagon so they could get out to Fort Lodgepole.

"Giving 'em the wagon? All right, it's yours to toss away if you want to. You're not shifting your supplies to my wagons or Haltmans', and all Rio has left is a two-wheeled cart."

"We got some pack horses."

"It's up to you. You'll have to make your own grub pile."

"That's what we intended, seh. It's not far to the Belle Fourche."

He didn't miss the look of satisfaction on Mixler's face as he turned to go. He had driven off the Jasons and McCraes. Reavley would be next, or Carson.

They set out, McCrae driving, an extra team tied to the end gate.

Relief at getting away brought Callie from her bed, and for an hour she rode in the seat beside her husband. They traveled all night with McCrae, Jason, and Jason's wife taking turns at driving while the riders ranged the country looking for Sioux. They camped

138

awhile at Big Muddy Springs, changed teams, and cut across roadless flats toward the southwest.

In the afternoon they sighted a freight outfit, a string of twenty wagons creeping northward along the Army road. The boss, a rough, redheaded man, said, "You're welcome to string along with my outfit as far as Tongue River Post. This outfit is Army contract supplies, and we were supposed to have a thirty-man escort from Lodgepole. Only there's nothing left at Lodgepole except ashes."

Johnny asked, "Indian attack?"

"No, they abandoned it, and the Injuns came along and set it afire. Moved north to Bozeman. But we'll get through. This here is Cheyenne country, and they're my in-laws. I got a Cheyenne squaw back at the South Fork." He looked inside the wagon at Callie McCrae. "You ain't a breed. No. Well, this country's pretty rough on a woman if she hasn't got a little Injun blood."

Returning to the trail herd, Johnny and his partners found the cattle bedded down along the bottoms of Eaglerock Creek. Reavley had abandoned his makeshift cart and was using pack horses.

"Gepp has been caring for your pack string," he said. "Y'know, this is the way to travel. On the loose with pack horses. Ground opens up in front of you, you got pack horses, you don't give a hoot. No flour, no beans, just live on meat straight like an Injun. I feel like I'd shed an anvil from around my neck. A man has to admit it — this was a hell of a trip to try with women and kids."

"Not too good down there, either," Johnny said, jerking his head toward the west.

"Injuns?"

"We didn't see any. Only long-off signal. I guess they'll get through."

"To Montana?"

"I wasn't thinking of that. Meant they'd find safety. But they'll be headed for the Yellowstone as soon as they can. Promised to meet 'em there in the fall. I'm cutting their cattle along with ours and driving them to Deadwood."

Reavley, after a second of surprise, laughed.

Johnny said, "You don't think Mix will let me take my cattle either, do you?"

"Remember how he tried to shoot our guts out last time?"

"I remember."

"There's only one way you'll take those cattle to Deadwood, and that's by driving 'em over the ground you've buried him in."

Big Bill said, "I can't see what difference it makes to Mixler. What if we do drive to Deadwood?"

"It makes this difference: The Deergrass country up in Montana was just thrown open from the Blackfoot treaty reserve. This herd will do a nice job of grabbing it all. Big outfits like the Diamond Bar and the Sixty-nine won't get a foothold. No, he's holding the herd together. He'll do it in spite of you, and in spite of hell."

It rained for two days, then the sun came out. The country had a bright, washed fragrance. The herd moved without dust. It was good to breathe and be

140

alive. José unwrapped his guitar from his slicker and sang. When Johnny Colt rode up he said, "Today we do not scout for the Sioux?"

"No time for it. We're not far from the Belle Fourche." He pointed it out, a purple-shadowed valley in the ouier distance, northwest. "Mixler'll never stop the herd. We'll have to start cutting our stuff now."

"How about their cattle?" he asked, meaning Jason's and McCrae's.

"Well, that'll take some thought. Maybe we'll do something about that at the last minute."

José, flashing his white teeth, slapped the gun at his waist. "Maybe drive them over hees grave?"

"And maybe he'll drive all of them nawth over *our* graves."

They worked easily through the morning, cutting Tom Mace's steers from the bunch, drifting them to one side, bringing them back toward the drag. In this manner, a third of the Mace stock had been bunched when Mixler learned of it and came at a gallop with other men stringing out at his heels.

There were five with him, headed by Star Glynn.

Mixler galloped almost atop Johnny Colt before bringing his horse around with a mean twist of the bridle. He barked, "Who said you could start cutting the herd?"

Johnny answered, "If you'll notice, this is all Rocking A stock."

"Why didn't you tell me you wanted your cattle cut? Your job is scouting for Indians."

Johnny Colt found a burr in his horse's mane and thoughtfully removed it. Without shifting his eyes, he could see Star Glynn edging to the left, his body to one side in a hip-out position that placed the butt of his gun where he wanted it. Ed Ward had moved the other way, but unlike Glynn, so slack and casual, he stood in the stirrups and kept his elbows pressed tightly against his body. He wondered which was faster, Glynn or Ward. Glynn, probably. He had that easy, don't-give-a-damn look, like José.

Johnny still picked cocklebur fragments. José and Big Bill were riding up from the drag. He wondered if this would be the showdown. He wished José and Bill would stay back. It was a good chance for Mixler, getting them all together at once, outgunned three to six.

Johnny tilted his head toward the blue summits of the mountains and drawled, "Them's the Black Hills yonder. Do you recollect when we joined it was understood that the Black Hills would be the end of our trail?"

"All right, make the Black Hills the end of the trail. If you have a fancy for Deadwood, why don't you start now?"

"Not without our cattle, seh."

Mixler was bent forward in his saddle, both hands braced on the pommel, a posture that accentuated the massive depth of his chest, the breadth of his shoulders. It placed his gun just back of his right hand.

"Not without your cattle? That's up to me. Everything's up to me. I'm running the herd."

142

José, coming to a stop, cried, "You mean you would take from us our cattle and drive them to —"

"Josie!" Johnny Colt cut him off. José would go too far. It would be playing into Mixler's hands. The showdown would come, but he, Johnny Colt, wanted to choose the time and place.

Glynn moved his horse, and Johnny shifted to match it, keeping Mixler between them.

Mixler shouted to José, "You got something on your mind, just say it straight out. This is as good a place to settle things as any."

Johnny said, "We just want our stock, the stock Tom Mace wanted driven to Deadwood."

"We're behind schedule. We should be across the Belle Fourche. I can't let you hold up the herd while you do your cutting."

Johnny laughed and shrugged. "If that's the way it is, why, that's the way it is." He lifted his hand in the Confederate cavalryman's salute. "I await your orders, seh."

"Same orders as ever. You keep tab on those Indians. We'll worry about cutting your stock."

CHAPTER
TWELVE

José cursed steadily under his breath as they drifted toward the bench country. He reined around and cried, "Was thees the Johnny Colt of old that I saw making wrinkles in his belly, bowing before that king of the gunmen? Was thees the Johnny Colt that shot Querno and Alderdice weeth two shots, bang-bang, in the hot dust of Guadalupe?"

Johnny asked, "You like to be buried here?"

"I will not be buried here. Was it not told to me by a gypsy in Tres Castillos that I would die reech and respected, amid the broad acres of my hacienda, to the music of my weeping peons and grandchildren, both by the hundreds?"

"Josie, you're good with that Sam Colt revolvin' gun. Your fame has spread far and wide, and I guess so has mine and Bill's. I'd be willing to brag a little and guess we would outdraw 'em, any three of us against any three of them. But while we got three of them, the other three would be getting three of us. According to my arithmetic, I'd say that left them in the majority. This is a republic, Josie, just like Mexico, and you know how republics are. The majority is a mighty potent force."

"You will then let them take our cattle."

"I didn't say that. It's just that we won't be able to do our job alone. We'll need Reavley and Carson and all the other men we can round up."

It was night. Johnny, lying in his blankets, could hear the regular snoring of Big Bill, but no sound came from José's bed.

After a long wait he said, "Josie, are you awake?"

"*Sí*. Awake thees long time thinking. We should not worry about what is burned on the sides of our cattle. Who cares in Deadwood, that camp of hungry men cut off by Sioux? When the times comes we will take our share, nine hundred, and drive toward Deadwood."

"I've been thinking the same thing. We'll talk it over with Reavley."

"Now?"

"Now."

"How about Bill?"

"Let him sleep. He's too big. Night or day, they could recognize a man as big as Bill. We could be just a couple of punchers on the night watch."

"*Sí*. They will be watching."

They moved quietly through the sleeping camp. The cattle were unusually quiet. It was a bad sign.

Johnny said, "Those cows got a run in their systems, and sometime they'll get it out. I'd hate to be in front of 'em when it happens."

They found the rope corral. The horse wrangler was taking a nap with a blanket over his head.

He woke up and said, "Oh, it's you boys. You taking a turn at night watch, or have you got a smell of Injuns?"

"Injuns," said Johnny. "Don't say anything. We don't want to stir the boys unless we have to."

The wrangler looked scared and helped them rope and saddle their horses. They rode to Reavley's camp, about three miles away. Pancake Jeffers was hunkered over a fire no bigger than his two hands, heating coffee in a sirup can. He jumped up at sound of the horses and leveled a Sharps rifle that had been lying beside him.

"Johnny Colt and Josie," Johnny said.

"Oh. By grab, you want to be careful how you come atop this camp at night. All the boys aren't as steady with their trigger fingers as I am."

"Where's Rio?" Johnny asked.

"He ain't here." Pancake had never got over his suspicion of them because they stayed in Mixler's camp.

"I can see that. Where is he?"

"Well — I guess he's yonder in the dry wash."

Pancake led them to the edge of the wash, the Sharps still in the bend of his arm.

"Rio!" he called in a low voice. "Rio, we got visitors."

The answer came from an unexpected direction. "Who is it?"

"Johnny and the Mex."

Rio was climbing the side. There was a click-click of metal as he lowered the hammer of a gun. "Tell 'em to wait there."

146

He had been carrying his boots. He wore no socks. He sat down and pulled the boots on his bare feet.

Johnny said, "You walk in some cactus that way, they'll hear you beller in Texas."

"My feet are so tough they could shoe me like a horse." He came the rest of the way. "What's gone wrong? You and Mix stir yourselves another batch of trouble?"

"No, same old batch he put to risin' back on the Platte. I'd guess he was well pleased with the way it was coming."

"It's not gone exactly to plan. He drove off McCrae and Jason like he wanted, but trading Tom Mace for the three of you was just like sand in the sugar."

"Think he tried to bushwhack Tom?"

Rio laughed. He didn't consider the question worth an answer.

José said, "This is once, Johnny, when you were wrong. In Maverly you said Mixler was not a shoots-in-the-back kind. Now you see he shoots in the back, the front or anywhere else to win."

Johnny said to Rio, "We're still heading for Deadwood, but it'll be a tough break to make alone. You better throw in with us. You and Wolf both."

"There's three of you, five of us. Five and three don't stack up too high against Mixler. He'd gun us down just like he tried to do the other side of Windham."

"Might be another way."

"How?"

"He expects his showdown with us at the Belle Fourche. We could make the break earlier, maybe about three days from now, when we reach that big bottom they call the Ironrod."

"You mean just cut a chunk out of this herd and start chasing 'em?"

"That's what I mean."

Reavley thought about it. Wolf Carson had come up in time to hear the end of the conversation and he said:

"I'll go. I've taken enough on this drive. Been kicked around enough. Been treated like white trash enough. Rather'n take any more, I'll hole up in the rocks and live like an Injun."

"All right." They were hard words for Reavley to say. He had set his mind on getting a chunk of the Deergrass, but the departure of Carson would have left him alone at Mixler's mercy. "How do you plan it? Our cut will be about three thousand."

"Thirty-six hundred. I promised McCrae."

"Thirty-six hundred, then. Will we just take them off the drag?"

"I'm not taking the drag. Our cattle have to be willing to travel through that Injun country. Noticed every morning there's one bunch hits out together led by an old brindle steer. That's our herd ready-made for us. When the time comes we'll just cut 'em loose and run 'em down the bottoms. Those cowboys eating dirt on the swing and the drag won't even notice. Wagons out ahead, Star Glynn and his bunch somewhere sleeping in the shade. Easy."

"Mix will follow. He'd follow us across the slag bottoms of hell."

"With all his men? That would mean abandoning the herd in Injun country."

"How many men will we have?"

"Jack Finch might go, and the horse wrangler. They both been having trouble with Mixler."

José said, "My countryman Gonzales already love me like a brother. Besides, I owe him the sum of twenty pesos, and how will he collect unless he comes along to Deadwood?"

CHAPTER
THIRTEEN

Returning, they found the camp asleep as they had left it. The day passed without an Indian smoke rising in the sky. It was hot, and dust again was pounded to drifting haze by the hoofs. At night they made their beds in some high sagebrush. The moon was so bright that Big Bill was able to make out passages in the book he carried with him, "How to Make One Hundred Thousand Dollars in the Cattle Business Out West."

Looking out above the book with dreamy eyes, Bill said, "I sure would like to turn these nine hundred cattle loose on the Deergrass and watch 'em multiply. Might be a favor if he wouldn't let us quit the herd."

José said, "Before you multiply them too fast, please to count the steers wearing our brand."

"Might be a favor to Tom. Listen to what this book says —"

"In Deadwood you sell the steer for feefty dollars, on the Deergrass for ten. Your book says drive to Deergrass, then I say your book is a fool."

"Now, the author takes care of *that* on page twelve. Listen."

While Bill read, Johnny watched the Haltman wagon. A candle burned inside and shadows moved against the

150

cloth top. One was Mixler, one Vern Haltman. And there was Ed Ward. Mixler kept talking, emphasizing his words with jerking movements of his head. It occurred to him that he could hear easily enough if he could creep beneath the wagon.

He gave up the idea. They would have sentries out.

Big Bill kept reading, squinting to make out words although he had committed many of them to memory. "And beware the buyer who offers double or treble the market price for your cattle, for he is certainly a charlatan."

José, lightly playing his guitar, said, "I once knew a man from Charley Town, he was not so bad. He was a stage driver." A smile touched his lips. "His wife, she was not so bad either. A little bit fat, maybe, but what is wrong weeth that?"

Johnny, still watching Haltman's wagon, asked, "How old was she?"

"Does a gentleman ask the age of a woman? Perhaps in Texas, but in Chihuahua —"

"I like 'em young myself. Young and slim, with black hair and color in their eyes."

"Ha, yes. If a man is in a beeg town weeth plenty of women, he can say, 'Take thees one away, she is too fat. Take thees one away, she is too thin.' But when a man has been out on the desert for three months, does he say these things? No. He asks one question: 'Is she a woman?' If the answer is yes, then that is pretty good."

"Tell me about that fat wife of the stage driver."

"Why should you laugh at her, this poor woman, old and fat with a wart on the end of her nose? Sitting around in an adobe town with no tree for forty miles, waiting for her husband, who is out driving a stage for a whole week at a time and never home. What kind of a man are you to laugh at her big jowels and the wart on her nose? You should be from Chihuahua and have some respect for women. Besides, she made a very good apple pie."

"Oh, hell," Bill said, and put the book away in his war sack.

The light in Haltman's wagon still burned, but the men seemed to have gone. The camp was quiet. There were the night sounds of cattle. Somewhere a cowboy was singing the endless verses of "The Rabble Soldier."

José wrapped his guitar, yawned, and rolled up in his blankets. Johnny, long awake, looked up at the stars.

The arid country had absorbed the rain, and now it was as though none had fallen. There was a scent of smoke from forest fires somewhere in the Black Hills. A slight veil of smoke magnified the stars. They seemed to be suspended scarcely a pistol shot overhead. The night herder, to the slow rhythm of his horse's hoofs, was singing:

> "I cry for rye whisky
> Wherever I roam,
> I'm an old rabble soldier
> And Dixie's my home."

Johnny had avoided Reavley all day. He didn't want to be seen talking to him. Mixler was no fool. He was wary as a wolf. He'd be quick to suspect. Now, with the camp asleep, he wanted to find Reavley and arrange some details with him.

The cowboy's song was closer now:

> "Oh, bring me cold lager
> And scrape off the foam,
> I'm an old rabble soldier
> And Dixie's my home."

The cowboy made a turn and the song receded. Johnny Colt dozed and was suddenly awake.

He lay on his back, with the hard prairie under him, looking at the sky. There'd been something — a sound, a movement. He listened. He could hear José breathing regularly, the snoring of Big Bill.

Several minutes went by. The cowboy's song had been engulfed in the vast prairie night. Distantly, an ember of the fire exploded, showering sparks.

He sat up. He noticed that his hand was closed on the butt of his pistol. He wondered how long he'd been holding it. His palm was sweaty. The camp was getting him. A few more days and he'd be losing control of his nerves. He wished he had a smoke. He felt his pockets for tobacco, found it, but didn't bother to roll one.

It was his imagination. No one had been prowling around. A couple of weeks in Deadwood was what he needed. A gallon of whisky and enough fiddle music to let him dance holes through his boot soles.

He was clothed, except for his boots. He pulled them on and, still not moving from his bed, strapped his gun around his waist. Then he realized someone was close, coming through the sage.

It should have alarmed him. It didn't. He spoke quietly. "Who's there?"

"Me." It was Lita.

Her voice brought that old topsy-turvy feeling to his abdomen. He got to his feet. He couldn't see her. Only the tall sage. Big Bill still snored, but José was awake, listening. He knew what José would be thinking. The low-minded Mex-Irish half-breed.

She was farther away than he thought. She whispered, "Here, Johnny," and he saw her, a slim shadow, crouched on one knee amid the sage.

She was frightened. The moon, shining brightly, revealed the rapid beat of an artery in her throat. It was a soft throat, tawny and smooth. It made him think of that girl, long ago, at the cantina. La Favorita, with the scarlet flower in her hair. It made him think of her more than that other girl, the blonde girl with her cool, pure loveliness. A man can't have everything. A man has to make his choice. And sometimes, if he's lucky, he can *take* his choice.

Her lips were slightly parted. Her eyes, wide and dark, kept on the move, hunting the shadows. She was afraid that someone had seen her leave the wagon and had followed her.

He said, "Don't be scared. We'll take care of things all right."

He thought she was going to back away. He took hold of her arm. It surprised him how small and soft it

154

was. A man forgets about women, living whole months and years in the rough land of men.

She whispered, "I had to find you. You can't stay here any longer."

"Here?" He motioned toward the immediate camp.

"You can't stay with the herd. You'll have to get away — tonight."

He hadn't much interest in danger. He kept thinking how small and young and pretty she was, and he had to force himself to concentrate on her words. "You heard that powwow in the wagon tonight?"

"Yes. They found out something about you. Something you're going to do. I tried to get closer, but Ellis came and I had to hide. You went somewhere last night, and Kiowa followed you. You had some sort of talk with Reavley. I heard that much."

He cursed through his teeth. He should have known Mixler would have someone watching them. They were fools to get horses from the remuda. He should have left the camp alone, on the quiet.

He said, "Yeah, I saw Rio. I talked to him about cutting his stock and moving it along with ours to Deadwood. What does Mix think he'll do about it? Just bushwhack *me*?"

"I'm not sure. He'll kill you. He or Star Glynn. I know it." There was fear in her voice. He liked the sound of it — a girl being scared for him.

He said, "And you don't want 'em to kill me?"

"Of course I don't! I came here, didn't I?"

A man would almost think she was angry, the straight way she stood, the intensity of her eyes as she

155

looked up at him. He could smell her hair. It had a fresh wind-and-sage odor. She was so close he had an impression of her body, its warmth and smoothness, and yet no part of her touched him.

She made a sudden move, and the thought that she was going made him grab her by the arms, just below her shoulders.

"Johnny!" She whispered his name and twisted from side to side. She was trying to get away but not trying hard enough. She wanted to get away, and she didn't want to. She was struggling against herself. "Johnny, they mustn't find me here!"

"Who mustn't find you here?"

"You know!"

She meant Mixler. He thought of that night he'd seen the two of them at the front of the wagon. It had been Mixler holding her that night, and she'd fought against *him*. Memory of it made him go tight inside with a cold dampness across his forehead.

His hands closed hard, his fingers sank into her flesh. He hurt her and that's what he wanted to do. She caught her breath and twisted, really trying to escape, but his strength kept her helpless.

"Johnny, you're hurting me!"

"You don't care anything about Mixler!" It wasn't a question, but a command. He was trying to tell her and himself that there'd never been anything between them.

"Let me go!"

"Answer me! You don't care anything for him!" He shook her back and forth. She'd unbraided her hair, getting ready for bed, and it fell in dark masses around her shoulders. In the day, with her hair pulled tightly into braids, she looked like a boy. There was nothing boyish about her now. He stopped shaking her. She leaned back and he had the feeling that she'd have fallen if he'd let go. She looked at him with a peculiar shot-animal expression in her eyes.

He whispered, "Answer me! You don't care anything about him. He's old enough to be your father. He has a wife back in Texas. He has a son as old as you are, do you know that?"

What difference did it make whether Mixler had a woman or ten women in Texas? What difference whether he was thirty years old, or thirty-five, or forty-five? This was the trail; this was the wild Northwest, and Mixler was a man. No matter how you hated him, Mixler was one hell of a man.

She said, sounding out of breath, "Why are you talking about him? What makes you think I want him? Have you been talking to Vern? He's always out watching me. He always thinks I'm sneaking out with Mixler."

"Aren't you?"

She sobbed, "No!"

"Oh, hell, why should you lie to me? It's none of my business, only I saw you one night — there in front of the wagon. You and Mixler. That was a long time ago. The other side of Windham."

"Oh." She seemed to have a hard time remembering. "*That* night. I hadn't been out with him. I was at Callie McCrae's. One of the boys found some eggs when we crossed Willow Creek and Daddy had made custard for her. Mix knew where I'd gone and waited for me. He knows I try to keep out of his way, so he's always hiding and waiting for me."

She whispered intensely, "You go ahead and ask Daddy if he didn't make the custard and if I didn't take it to her."

"No, I don't need to. I believe you."

He let her go, and she didn't seem to notice. She said fiercely, "I hate him! He smells like sweat and horses. I could smell him in the dark when he was there, waiting for me. Sometimes I hide until he goes away. I hate him!"

He felt ashamed. All he could think of to say was: "I'm sorry."

"Why did you talk to me that way?"

"I told you I was sorry."

He was thinking that if he went to Deadwood, it would mean leaving her behind. He didn't want to leave her with Mixler. Not even though three of her brothers were along.

She'd moved away from him. Something made her eyes once more dart around the shadows. "I have to go," she whispered.

"Lita, wait a second."

"No. They'll notice I'm gone. You know what Vern will say. He goes crazy mad when he thinks I'm seeing anybody."

He started after her anyway. She ran. For the first time he noticed she was barefoot.

He stood for several seconds after she was out of sight around the wagon. His own danger again asserted itself. It occurred to him that if Kiowa had been watching last night, he'd be watching again tonight. He'd have seen her. He'd carry the news straight to Mixler.

A whisper in the sagebrush made him spin around, drawing his gun with a movement that was practically reflex.

The smiling voice of José said, "Pull the trigger, señor, and you will be shooting away all your chances of collecting my indebtedness, a total of feefty thousand dollars and some odd cents. I was sleeping and I dreamed you had a visitor. The dream was so real I could almost see it was a girl with no shoes on. Perhaps you have friends you do not tell your dear José about?"

"Go to hell." He put the gun back. "They know we talked with Reavley."

"She told you that?"

"Yes."

"That was why she was here?"

"Yes, damn it!"

"Eh, too bad. But do they know *what* we said at Reavley's?"

"I think that snaky breed crawled in and heard us."

"Kiowa?"

"Yes, that's what they had the powwow about. She thinks they have Star and his boys out to kill us."

"Good! For too long have I sat quiet and done nothing. We had better wake Big Bill. He is a good man in a fight. With a Winchester, I would not trade him even for you."

"All right, wake him, but keep him here."

"You mean to go alone? This is the time for steeking together. Even a bushwhacker thinks twice before shooting at the three of us, back to back, looking in all directions."

"They won't shoot. Not tonight. Not with those cattle ready to jump."

He left José and walked through tall sage, coming around behind the wagons. He met no one. Cowboys, fagged after dawn to dusk in the saddle, snored in their beds. It was not yet time for the second watch.

The fire glowed under a coating of ash; coffee thudded in the big black pot. He decided to pour a cup. It was scalding hot, and the steam looked like smoke in the night chill.

The girl was in her wagon, watching him. He could not see her, but he knew. He was strong on hunches. He became aware of someone else. A moving shadow — a slight sound. Someone was back of the wagon, hidden by a saddle heap.

He finished the coffee, rolled a cigarette, lighted it with a twig from the fire. He yawned and walked that way. When he was by the rear wheel he turned casually with his gun in his hand and said:

"You're a dead man if you move."

His words brought the man suddenly to his feet. It was Kiowa Jim.

Kiowa had reached by instinct for his gun. He checked himself.

Johnny said, "Keep your hands clear of that gun. Don't talk."

160

He plucked Kiowa's gun from its holster. Kiowa watched him without speaking, apparently without breathing, only his eyes in movement. He seemed smaller than usual. He was wearing moccasins. At night he looked more like a fullblood than a half-breed.

"We'll walk now, Kiowa. Out of camp. Over yonder."

He knew what the breed thought — that it was going to be a one-way walk. He let him go on thinking it. They moved away from the wagons, beyond the firelight, through sage that grew to their waists.

A night herder rode up within a few hundred yards. His horse made a slight rustle in passing the Sage clumps. He sang, very softly:

"They say I drink whisky,
My money's my own,
I'm an old rabble soldier
And Dixie's my home."

Johnny said, "I notice you've taken to wearing moccasins."

"What's wrong with moccasins?"

"Nothing, especially if you aim to sneak around and listen. Y'know, Kiowa, I paid a visit to the other camp last night, and all the while I was there I had the most peculiar feeling that somebody had crawled up on his belly like a snake to hear what I said. That couldn't have been you?"

"I sleep. All the time in my blankets."

"It's no use, Kiowa. You were there. You were on watch tonight and saw the girl visit me, too. Now you're to the point where you know too much. I guess I'd be better off if you never talked to Mixler again."

Kiowa cried, "Wait!" The eyes he turned on Johnny were sharp from fear. "What good would I be to you dead?"

"That ain't the question. What good are you alive? You think up a couple of good reasons why I ought to leave you all in one piece without leaks."

"I'll get out of camp. I'll catch a horse and head for Deadwood or Maverly."

Johny laughed and said, "I think I could send you a lot farther."

"I'll go to Mixler. You tell me what to say. I tell him. You listen outside. If I don't —"

"No, that's not good enough either." He prodded him with the gun. They kept walking. "Tell me what went on inside Haltman's wagon tonight."

After a few seconds of indecision he started to talk, using quick words, Indian style, emphasizing like an Indian with jerks of his head.

"He thinks at Ironrod Coulee, tomorrow, you do something."

"Keep talking."

"I don't know any more. I wasn't inside. Ed Ward he was inside. I tried to hear, but damn, no."

Kiowa tried to stop.

"Walk," Johnny said, ramming him with the gun.

It was a quarter-hour walk to Reavley's camp, where Fred Jardine was on watch.

162

"Saw you two-three hundred yards off," Jardine said, fingering his Winchester. "What the hell you doing with the breed?"

"He was in the coulee listening last night."

Jardine cursed. "Has he told Mix?"

"Of course."

"Now what?"

"Why, we'll have to move fast. We can't wait for the Ironrod. Mix will never let us get there."

"Figure we can cut and drive tomorrow?"

"Not a chance. He'll be watching us like a hungry buzzard. It'll have to be tonight."

They roused the camp. After hearing his story, Reavley cried, "Why, if we try to cut that herd tonight they'll run from here to Jericho!"

"That's all right with me, if they go through Deadwood on the way."

Reavley shrugged, laughed, and said, "What can we lose?"

Wolf Carson yipped. "Deadwood, hyar I come! Damn, I could do with a nip o' that city life, and by what I hear, Deadwood's even worse'n Cheyenne." And the old fellow started waltzing with an imaginary dance-hall girl, singing in his tuneless voice a song he'd picked up on the trail:

> "But look out for the Sioux
>   And their tomahawk kills,
> They will take home your scalp
>   From the dreary Black Hills."

Johnny said, "Keep Kiowa entertained. I'll go yonder and hunt out the boys."

He ran most of the way back to camp. He stopped short of the wagons to get his breath and look around. Everything seemed to be quiet, but as he started past the cook wagon, Mixler's voice stopped him.

"Where you been?"

Mixler stood with his back against the high front wheel, in partial shadow. He was not alone. With him were Rasmussen, Ed Ward, and Star Glynn.

"Quite a reception," Johnny said.

Mixler repeated with a savage note, "Where you been?"

"I needed the night air."

"You been seeing those yellow turncoats about splitting the herd."

"This country's pretty wide and free."

"My herd isn't free. And any man that tries to split it is asking for one thing. He's asking for two hundred and fifty grains of lead in his guts."

"You have enough guns." He wondered why Mixler hadn't just killed him as he walked, up. He realized then that the herd had saved him. Mixler wouldn't risk a stampede.

Mixler said, "But you can go. The boys will escort you from camp." He turned and said quietly to Star Glynn, "How about the big fellow and the greaser?"

"Billy's still watching 'em."

Johnny laughed and said in a loud voice, "No guts! You're bushwhacking me like you did Tom Mace!"

Mixler flinched. He shot a glance at Haltman's wagon.

The door was open, blackness inside. You couldn't tell whether the girl was there, but it was plain enough that Mixler thought she was there.

Johnny said, "Y'know, if I was a woman out to pick a mate for myself, I'd sure as hell want one like you that hired five or six men to shoot his chief rival in the back."

The words and the smiling contempt behind them made Mixler straighten with every muscle solid in his bull-moose body.

Johnny said, "O'course she's listening. I imagine she's comparing the two of us right now. Can't you guess what's running through her head? There's Johnny Colt, no more brains than to walk into a deadfall. But there's Mixler, he's a real leader of men. A little bit yellow, o'course, but still a leader of men, telling those hired guns just what to do. It always beats me, Mix, how a natural-born general like you stayed home from wah. I guess, though, you were needed worse keeping your cattle together in Texas."

Mixler stood straight with his legs braced, arms at his sides, fists doubled. He opened his hands slowly, and slowly closed them. He didn't look at Haltman's wagon again. He forced himself to look straight at Johnny Colt, though he must have sensed she was listening, and that others had awakened and were listening, too.

Fury made his face look hollow, accentuated his jawbone, his cheeks, the tendons and corded muscles of his neck. He moved his lips to speak, but no sound came. He lifted his right hand, wiped his mouth hard with the back of it.

Then he said in a raw whisper, "You think you have me because I wouldn't dare shoot — because those cattle are ready to jump."

Johnny laughed, putting in all the derision he could.

Mixler loosened his gun belt. Holding it by the buckle, he let the gun-weighted holster swing around his body. It dropped, and he stood with his hands on his hips unarmed.

He said, "All right, you're the man with guts. Or do you have guts? Maybe you've just stood behind the barn and practiced grabbing that gun out of the holster."

Johnny pulled his belt loose, started wrapping it around the holstered gun. Mixler, with arms thrust forward, charged him.

Johny dropped the gun, tried to bend and pivot. The wagon was behind him. He moved to his left. He was trapped by the front wheel. He came to a stop with his boots set and swung a left and right to Mixler's jaw.

Mixler took both of them and came on in his bull rush. He carried his lighter adversary in front of him.

Johnny half fell. One shoulder struck the wheel. His head snapped, and the back of it came in contact with the iron tire.

It drove blackness and lightning flashes of pain through his head. He realized that he was down. He fought to regain his feet before the man could trample him under his boots. He was on hands and knees for a timeless interval. His legs were paralyzed, his veins seemed to flow with something as heavy as quicksilver.

Actually he was down little more than a couple of seconds. Mixler had backed up to charge. When he came, Johnny, half standing, met him. He fell forward, wrapped both arms around his waist.

Blows rained on him. He refused to be smashed loose. With blind, desperate strength, with his shoulder in Mixler's abdomen, he lunged. He carried the man three steps. There Mixler's right spur caught in a tuft of bunch grass, and they fell backward.

Mixler would have wrestled, but Johnny Colt twisted free.

He stood. He was able to see again, able to stand, able to walk.

Mixler rolled over with a quickness remarkable in a man of his size and rushed with massive, clublike rights and lefts.

Johnny managed to ride them out. He waited his chance. He made a half pivot, set his heels, and came back around with a left hook. He kept the blow close to his body. Behind it lay the strength of arm, back, and leg. All he had was put in the apex of that one punch.

It snapped Mixler's head to one side. His hat was gone. His eyes were out of focus. Johnny Colt measured him with a right, and smashed him to the ground.

He rolled and came to a crouch. His eyes were like those of a steer under the hammer. Blood ran from his lips. His belt with his holstered gun was near, on the ground. He grabbed it and lunged. The Colt pistol was like a blackjack at the end of the doubled belt.

Johnny tried to retreat and fend it off. The gun's weight, coming with terrific force, smashed through his upraised arm and clubbed him on the ground.

Mixler stopped above him, spread-legged, reared his big body high, and swung again, but Johnny rolled and got his head and shoulders behind the high rear wheel.

Mixler cursed and tossed the bludgeon aside. He sprang with one hand clutching the wheel and repeatedly drove the heel of his right boot to the side of Johnny's head.

José and Big Bill, coming on the run, reached the wagon and saw their partner, bloody-faced, with his arms wrapped around his head, under the wagon, and Mixler, breathing heavily, strapping his gun back around his waist.

"What is this?" José drew up with his right hand swinging loose and his body turned to bring the butt of his Colt out ready for the cross draw. His eyes, moving quickly, noticed Johnny's gun on the ground, while Star Glynn and his men were ranged around. "You shoots-in-the-back! You hold a gun on him and beat him!"

Mixler laughed. He laughed and wiped blood from the corner of his mouth and laughed again. The sight of Johnny Colt, battered and bleeding, made him feel better than he had in days.

"You think so, greaser? Well, take another look. There's not a gun out of the holster. I beat him with my fists. I could have killed him, but I didn't. You put that down to charity." His eyes traveled to the wagon. The three Haltman boys were outside. Lita, a shadow

168

behind them, was listening. He turned back, looked again at Johnny, who was still only half conscious. He hitched up his pants, again calling attention to those stud-horse legs. "Take him with you. Saddle your stock and get out of camp. I'll give you one hour. One hour." He lowered his voice. "If you're here at the end of an hour, I won't shoot you. I'll hang you. I'll prop a wagon tongue over the hoops of that wagon and hang you."

CHAPTER
FOURTEEN

"I can walk," Johnny said, and elbowed José out of the way. He read an expression in Big Bill's eyes. "Don't do anything. It's like the man said. I was licked."

His left cheek and the lobe of his left ear were cut by Mixler's spur and boot heel. Bits of grass had stuck in the smeared and thickened blood.

He took a second to steady himself with one hand on the high wagon box. His gun and belt were still where he'd dropped them. He picked them up, started to draw the hammer to half cock so he could revolve the cylinder and see if it were still loaded.

"Just strap it on!" Mixler said. "Nobody unloaded it."

"Thank you, seh." His eyes swept the camp, making a brief tally of the men around them. He couldn't see them all. There were others out in the shadow. "You'll let us take our horses."

"Yes, take your horses and get out." He called to Ellis Haltman, who was coming from the wagon, "Go yonder and see to it that shifty wrangler don't give 'em any except their own."

"You mean just theirs, or Tom Mace's?"

"Theirs *and* Tom Mace's."

Back at their camp, Johnny lay propped on his elbows while Big Bill, working with blunt, gentle fingers, cleaned off his face with a dampened rag. Bill finished by sticking thin slices of chewing tobacco around the spur cuts, which still oozed blood.

"Spurs!" Johnny said. "Revelation, sort of. Lets a man know how a horse feels."

"I'd kill a man that treated a horse that way."

Johnny laughed and said, "Now you're putting me back in the class of Dave Jason."

"What do you mean?"

"You remember the old lady saying, 'Ain't it enough we saved Paw and the horses!'"

"I'd have killed him, only —"

"The hell you would have. You might have tried. But winning in this camp is like beating a Dodge City monte game. You need more'n luck. You need outside help."

José went over to the rope corral, returning a few minutes later, mounted, leading two saddled horses and a pack horse, and driving six more. That left one missing — a big chestnut gelding.

Johny mentioned the horse and was told that Pecos was riding him.

"All right, you get these things together and I'll find him. I'm not leaving a good horse for Mixler, even if Pecos does count him one of his string."

He mounted and set off on a course that took him among the wagons. The camp was quiet. He heard a soft hoof thud as a rider came out of the darkness and dismounted by the fire. It was Pecos.

Johnny laughed and said, "Well, I'm damned! I was just starting out to find you. I'll be needing that chestnut horse. We had a little ruckus. Mixler's running us out of camp."

Pecos stared at his cut-up face and said, "Sure. I'll pull my leather off him." Using a folded piece of gunny sack to grab its handle, he lifted the coffeepot. "Better have a cup in farewell. Look at it! Now, *there's* some coffee that'll last you for many a mile. Thick as N'Orleans sorghum."

Johnny said, "No," and then he said, "Well, maybe I will have a cup."

Pecos held it out for him. Johnny had dismounted and started around, leading his horse. The horse pulled so suddenly he almost got free. Someone had startled him. An instant later he saw a tall, spare man crouched behind a barrel that Daddy Bearsign had lifted down from the wagon. The man was Ed Ward.

Ward knew he'd been seen. He stood up very slowly. His hands were low, close beneath the twin Colts tied down to his skinny thighs.

Johnny said, "Waiting for me, Ed?"

Ward didn't answer. He was tense, his body hunched slightly forward.

Johnny went on, "I reckon you're the one that had the job of killing Tom Mace. Y'know, I'd have gone for you there in Maverly, but Tom asked me not to. If you want me, Ward, now's your time."

"Mixler'd kill a man that fired a gun tonight."

He pretended to turn away, then, as though released from a spring, he straightened with both hands coming up from the holsters.

But Johnny Colt had not been caught by the maneuver. He seemed slow and casual. He drew with a quarter pivot, the Colt leveling itself through its own momentum, his forearm braced against his hip. He hesitated the fraction of time needed to freeze on his target, and pulled the trigger.

Concussion hit the long night quiet with a sudden roar.

Johnny felt the rock of the gun in his hand. Ward fired at almost the same instant. Bullet lead whipped the air close across his chest. Gun flame, knifing across the darkness, momentarily blinded him. He took two steps around the wagon, glimpsed Ward's shadow, and fired again.

Ward was already hit. He'd limber-legged it around the barrel, the guns dangling at the ends of his long arms. The second bullet knocked him off his feet.

Johnny kept going and was caught in gunfire from two directions. He grabbed the wagon spokes and pulled himself back. They had him surrounded. Suicide spot. His horse, startled, tried to run, tripping on the bridle. He rammed his gun away, dived and got hold of the reins with one hand, a stirrup with the other.

Bullets tore the sod under him. He was holding to the off side and that added to the horse's terror. He kept hold of the stirrup. He was being dragged. His legs were under the horse's belly. Hoofs struck him in the backs of his thighs. For the space of three or four seconds all he could do was hold tight. Then, with a desperate grab, he got hold of the horn and pulled himself to the animal's back.

He was now fifty or sixty yards away with darkness covering him. He got the bronc stopped. He turned around. He poked empty cartridge cases from the magazine and reloaded.

They were still shooting. Over the crash of explosions he could hear the voice of José calling his name. He cupped his hands and answered.

He circled toward their camp. Gunfire ceased, but there was another sound, a rumble like thunder.

A man in camp shouted, "Stampede!"

The herd was in movement. By moonlight he could see the first rise of dust, the shine of moving horns, the dark backs of cattle, rolling like the sea.

The fight was forgotten. Men ran toward the rope corrals. No time for saddles. Content with a bridle or hackamore, they mounted bareback.

The thunder grew. Baffled by echo and darkness, the herd came straight toward the sounds that had alarmed them.

Johnny thought of the girl. He spurred toward the wagon. His horse veered from the fallen body of Ed Ward. He called, "Lita!" She answered him from off in the dark. She was already out and riding.

José called to him, ran over, a gun still in his hand, got hold of his stirrup. His teeth flashed white against his dark skin. "They are coming, those cows! Perhaps they weel run all the way to Deadwood, no?"

"That's a good thought. Where's Bill?"

The big fellow ran up, leading a saddle horse and pack horse with one hand, a Winchester, Colt, and cartridge belt in the other.

"Hey! It looks to me like they were headed this way." His high-pitched, accusing voice sounding out of place against the rising thunder of the herd. "We got to get out of here."

"And leave half our outfit? To hell with that. They'll split at the wagons. We'll let 'em roll by and pick the bunch we want for Deadwood. We'll pick the ones that act like antelope."

The main body of the herd was swinging slightly to the northeast. From down the knoll riders were on the gallop, whooping, firing six-shooters, trying to mill the leaders.

Johnny tied his bronc to the wagon and waited with his rifle. José was beside him. "Where's Bill?"

"Working with the horses."

Johnny called, "That's good enough. Turn the rest loose."

"Like hell. A horse is worth too much money." He came over breathing hard and asked, "Will we be able to turn 'em?"

"We won't turn 'em, but we'll split 'em. Looks like the main chunk of the herd was over yonder."

They waited a quarter minute as the herd roared closer. One bunch had already gone past to the north. Its dust rolled in a thick blanket, making it hard to breathe. They saw cattle veering off from the wagons. Others closed in, a dense, walleyed, terrified mass.

Johnny picked out a steer, put the Winchester to his shoulder, and fired. It was a snap shot, for there was no light to see the sights, but the .44 slug hit and the steer went down, horns first, its hindquarters rolling high.

"I hope that's not a Rocking A."

"No!" José shouted. "Keel Mixler's. This is like shooting Apaches, no?"

Soon there was no time for talking. They fired as fast as they could work the levers of the Winchesters. The guns grew too hot to hold. They tossed them aside as the mass of beef rolled onward, and used six-guns.

There were cattle down and cattle lunging over them, falling, being trampled, building into a heap beyond the wagons. Cattle rolled past on each side. One big steer came straight on, crashed the wagon box, fell beneath. Kicking and bawling, it got up, almost upsetting the wagon.

José cried, "A wager, señor! I will ride heem for one hundred dollars!"

Johnny's answer was drowned in the crashing guns.

They reloaded and fired blindly. Gun flames looked ruddy through air too thick to breathe, and suddenly there was nothing left — only the bawl of fallen ones, the drifting layers of dirt through which, now and then, one could see an outline of the moon.

"We are still here," said José. "We live, we breathe. Did I not say I would die reech and respected in the midst of my acres and my grandchildren in Chihuahua?"

176

They rode, following the herd. Here and there were strays wandering and bawling, but the main body of cattle still kicked up dust to the northeast.

Two riders crested a rise, and even from an eighth of a mile off Johnny knew one was Wolf Carson.

"Wolf!" he called, and they galloped up. The man with him was Al Geppert.

"Oh, it's you boys," Wolf said. "Well, thanks be to glory. We heard that shooting and saw the stampede and figured they'd shot you first and tromped you in the ground afterward. I see you even got out with your grub."

"Most of it. Where's Rio?"

"Yonder." Wolf jerked his head toward the upcountry. "You want me to bring him in?"

"No. You better come along with us. We'll start cutting out a chunk of beef."

"Say, this was made to order. You didn't make it to order, did you?"

There were strays on all sides of them. Some of them had started to graze.

Geppert said, "How about these?"

"No. This is off the drag. We'll need fast travelers if we expect to outrun Mixler and Sitting Bull both on the way to Deadwood."

They picked up a couple of hundred that were still bunched at the edge of jack timber on a hillside. There were other hundreds. Their herd was beginning to take shape. In an hour they met Rio Reavley, Pancake, and Fred Jardine working a ridge from the southwest.

"How many you got?" Johnny asked.

"I haven't tallied. Maybe twelve hundred."

"We'll pick up three or four hundred more riding straight east. That ought to give us thirty-one or thirty-two, hundred, total. If we get two thousand into the Black Hills at mining-camp prices, I'll not complain."

Reavley asked, "Where's Gonzales and the horse wrangler?"

"They'd have come, but how's a man to find them? Main thing is to put some miles under us before daylight."

Their cut of the beef was still willing to travel. Riding hard, shouting, swinging goads, they kept them at a trot up miles of coulee into steepening country. The high prairie was now behind. Here there were round-topped hills broken by dikes of volanic rock, black-patched with scrub pine.

The coulee forked, and forked again. They drove across slide rock and knee-high bramble to a bench terrace that ran for miles north and south, fronting the first great ridge of the Black Hills.

Dawn, in streaks of pink and yellow, silhouetted the summits. Dust still hovered in a fine cloud below — dust that first looked like gray fog and then turned the color of corn meal as the sun struck it.

The riders stopped. Some of them swapped saddles. They rolled smokes and had a few words before going on.

"Can you see them?" José asked, riding to a stop beside Johnny Colt. "I look and look, but what I think are cattle become only dancing specks in front of my eyes."

"Trouble with you, you been hitting the prune barrel in Daddy Bearsign's wagon."

"I have tasted not one drink since leaving Maverly, which is more than I can say for some men who come from visiting the Haltmans' smelling of fine Kentucky bourbon."

"The herd's yonder. No, 'way yonder. That main bunch swung in a big half circle. Why, they ended up farther west than they started."

After long watching, they could see that the herd was in movement. Cowboys were at work, rounding them up. It would be a big job. Mixler would have the tough choice of letting this thirty-one hundred go to Deadwood, or letting the main herd graze and scatter, with maybe a third part of them ending in one of Sitting Bull's cooking pots.

Johnny rubbed out the coal of his cigarette and spat on the blackened end before throwing it aside. They were in pine country, where fire could race a mile in a matter of minutes.

He said, "We better get moving. Get to Deadwood before Calamity Jane and Madame Mustache drink up all the liquor."

"Who are they?"

"Women, and that's just your style. How about it, Josie? You made love to a woman with a wart on her nose, and that fat widow in Chihuahua weighed three hundred pounds. You ever try one with a mustache?"

"If there is such in Deadwood, ask me that question twenty-four hours after I ride in town."

The drive went on all day, along the bench, across a vast mountain shoulder, and finally down through rock and pine to the depths of Ironrod Coulee.

A stream flowed in the bottom, clear and cold. In its deep riffles one could see the darting, grayish shapes of fingerling trout. It was mining country, prospected before Sitting Bull left the Agency, and shallow placer pits had been sunk every few hundred yards in the bench gravel.

"We'll camp here," Johnny said.

Darkness settled more rapidly here than on the plains. They found dry quaking aspen and built a little fire. It burned almost without smoke. They drenched it as soon as they'd made coffee and doughgods.

The bottoms were damp, growing lush with grass, but after a hot day the pines on the higher mountainsides gave out a dry, burned smell. Sunset was very red, with purples grading into violets, a coloration due to distant prairie and forest fires.

They sat around the dead fire, talking a little, listening. Rio got up and kicked the stiffness out of his legs. It was quite dark. They could hear him digging cartridges from his war sack.

"There'll be trouble tonight," he said.

"I doubt it." Johnny sounded sleepy. He lay on his back with clasped hands under his head, looking at the stars. "He'll wait, Mixler will. He don't go around just shooting off powder for the hell of it. He'll see where we're going, and then he'll go ahead and lay a nice cross-fire ambush, by good strong daylight, so's those gunmen can get us in the fine notch of their sights."

José said, "Now, thees puts my mind at ease. When I am killed, I want done a nice, neat job."

"Just the same," Rio said, "I'm watching the rocks."

"Sure. We'll split the night in half. That all right?"

Reavley, Geppert, and Jardine took the first watch. Johnny slept. When Jardine came down about midnight he sat up before a word was said. His boots were stiff from cold. He pulled them on and commenced working life into the leather.

"Cold night and a hot day, that's my meat. If I ever settled down I'd find me a place in the edge of the mountains."

"This night might end up by being a hot one."

"See anything?"

"Man scouting the camp."

Johnny cursed under his breath. "Maybe it was an Injun."

"That's what I thought, but he wasn't. I sneaked along and got up to a couple hundred steps, but he had a horse cached in the pines and rode off. He didn't use the off side like an Injun. I have a hunch it was Evas Williams."

"How long ago?"

"About an hour."

José was awake, and heard what was said. He dressed and walked out with his Winchester in the crook of his arm. "Should I wake Big Bill?"

"Let him sleep. He ate the drag on this herd all day. He earned it."

The remainder of the night passed without incident. They started driving the herd at the first gray sign of dawn. They were balky and wanted to graze, and it took hour of hard riding to get them in steady movement, across meadow bottoms, through brush, through rocky narrows.

Night had left a chill in the valley. Then the sun pierced its depths, and suddenly it was hot. Johnny Colt's teeth had been chattering; now sweat made his shirt cling to his back. Riding, shouting, swinging the rope goad had made him forget the danger of ambush. He remembered it now, and turned his horse up a deer trail that zigzagged through rock and timber to the north rim.

After a quarter hour he stopped to let his horse breathe. Mountain summits covered with forest rose to the east. At one place he could see a switchback trail terminating at a series of chalky-looking scars. Those were dumps extending downhill from the mouths of tunnels where some wandering prospector had taken his chance on Indians while exploring the outcrop of gold quartz vein.

He found himself whistling a tune and for a while he couldn't remember what it was. It was the one old Wolf Carson was singing and waltzing to the other night.

> There's loafers and tinhorns
>   Of 'most every plight
> On the go from Cheyenne
>   By day and by night;
> With rum and rye whisky

Loaded plumb to the gills,
Each day they ride off
For the dreary Black Hills.

A rider slowly climbed the far side. His manner in the saddle told him it was José.

Johnny kept riding, following a contour of the mountain, traveling at the same rate as José until he dropped from sight in a rocky draw.

The sun by then was almost at the zenith. It reflected from the bare rock, hot in a man's eyes. Johnny dismounted, hunkered in the shade of some wind-twisted scrub pine. He had moved far ahead of the herd. Now all he had to do was wait for it to catch up — wait, and watch for the movement that would tell him of pursuit.

By slow degrees, his eyes swept the vast country beneath him. When the wind was right he could hear the bawling cattle, the "Hi-up! Hi-up" shouts of men. But for the most part the country was held by a vast silence, broken only by the cries of veering eagles, and beneath, like part of the silence, the perpetual roar of wind currents through evergreens.

He was hungry. His eyes hurt. He closed his eyes to rest them, dozed for a few seconds. Looking again, he caught a flash of movement far across the valley.

A man on foot, tiny from distance, was climbing.

It wasn't José. José had long before reached one of the higher mountain levels. A second man, also on foot, perhaps a quarter mile to the west, was just disappearing in timber.

The timber grew in sparse strips, and he should have reappeared a few seconds later, but he didn't. He'd stopped there. Now both of them were out of sight. Suddenly he realized that José was coming from above, horseback, following a trail where talus rock sloped from the face, heading directly into ambush.

He cupped his hands and shouted. José did not look up. He shouted again and again, but José remained bent forward in his saddle, eyes on the treacherous descent.

Johnny drew his six-shooter, held it flat to a reflecting surface of rock, and fired.

José still rode as the echoes pounded away. Then, after what seemed to be a long wait, he jerked erect and looked. It had taken that long for the sound to reach him.

He'd turned and was looking, but about thirty degrees too far to the west. Johnny slipped off his shirt and swung it in high arcs, trying to reveal his position, but it did no good. Then, with a catlike, rolling movement, José dropped from the saddle, landing on all fours. Somehow he'd drawn the Winchester from its scabbard as he fell. He fired the instant he touched the ground. Johnny could see the spurt of powder smoke, and two other gun smokes from the timber, all before a report could be heard.

José was on his stomach. Without lifting himself more than a few inches off the ground, he moved from one rock cover to the next. From his high vantage place

Johnny could see every move he made, though José's movements were not visible to the men down the slope.

Johnny mounted and picked his way downhill. In timber, he had only brief glimpses of the battle across from him. He could no longer tell where José was, though the brittle cracking of gunfire still came, each shot multiplied by echoes that chased it like rapid handclaps.

As he neared bottom, a bullet stung the rocks five or six feet to his right and whined off with a vicious discord.

He should have expected it, but it had come as a surprise. His movement was pure reflex. He spurred, doubled over, his body behind the horse, his rifle in his hands, as more bullets flew around him.

Jack pine ripped at him, hid him from view. He dismounted, let the bridle drag. Squatting on his heels, he had a quick look around. A rock reef now separated him from his attackers. He reached it, clambered up its rough surface to the crest. Belly down, propped on elbows, he had a look at the other side.

There was a feed gulch, steep, timbered. Gun smoke ascended and drifted languidly on the hot air. He glimpsed movement below and to the right. A man was crawling on all fours. He aimed and fired with one movement, and saw the grayish shower of dirt as his bullet tore under the target. He fired again, again, as fast as his hand could operate the lever of the rifle, at the man as he scrambled through deadfalls.

He didn't wait any longer. He wanted to warn Reavley back at the herd.

He slid back down the reef, found his horse, rode around the slope, staying in timber, and came out with a view of the bottoms.

The herd was half a mile away. Only the lead steers were in view. Jardine and Reavley, hearing gunfire, had stopped. Reavley saw him and brought his gun up.

"It's me — Johnny!"

Reavley waited, watched. Having made sure it was indeed Johnny, he started up the valley at a gallop.

A gun cracked from high among the rocks. Reavley was hit. The bullet went through him and pounded gray dust from the earth beyond. He stayed with his horse for a second, then dived forward to the ground.

The ambusher fired again, aiming at Jardine. Jardine had whirled his horse around. The horse reared, and that saved him.

Johnny, on a low shoulder of bank, turned and saw the man hunkered, levering a third cartridge into his rifle. Even at 250 yards he could tell who it was. Star Glynn.

Johnny had no time to aim. He took a snap shot. It hit a couple of yards short of the mark with a shower of dirt.

Glynn shot at almost the same instant, but closeness of the bullet made him miss. Then he rolled over and was gone from sight.

Cursing, Johnny chased him with another bullet. He kept levering the Winchester until it was dry, trying for a lucky hit as Glynn was here and there visible, escaping around the mountain.

Johnny turned his horse, climbed, found a game trail. Giving free rein to the horse, he grabbed .44 cartridges from his belt and fed them into the Winchester magazine.

When steepness made the horse lose footing, he sprang off and climbed. He ran, vaulting over obstructions, climbing higher and higher. He didn't glimpse Star. He stopped with his lungs splitting for air. For a second he was dizzy. He lay with one cheek pressed against a sun-hot piece of slide rock while he got his breath. Then he sat up and recovered his bearings.

He could see the heap of logs where the ambusher had placed himself. The herd was all under his gaze. Lead steers, frightened by gunfire, had turned back. There was some jam-packed milling, horns tossed high.

Reavley lay face down, position unchanged. The sun raised a metallic gleam from the barrel of his rifle where it had fallen in low buck brush.

Big Bill had come up on the far side of the herd, and now the press of cattle had pinned his horse against the canyon wall. Johnny shouted to him, but the bawling of the herd covered his voice. Back on the drag were Pancake and Al Geppert. He couldn't see Wolf Carson.

He heard his name called, looked across, saw José riding downhill. All clear, he was signaling.

Johnny gave up on Glynn, returned to his horse, and met José in the bottom. "They bushwhacked Reavley, did you notice?"

"I noticed," José whispered through his teeth. "It was Star Glynn? Someday I theenk I will kill him. You hear? That is a promise. Someday I will kill him."

CHAPTER
FIFTEEN

They dug a grave as best they could without shovels, wrapped Reavley up in his blankets, and buried him with his hat over his face. The grave had only been a couple of feet deep, so they heaped it with slab rock. Afterward they stood in silence, uncomfortable, looking from one to another.

Finally José cleared his throat and said, "Señores, I know no prayer in English, but my dear mother in Chihuahua taught me many in Spanish. I had a good home. I was not always a drifting saddle bum. Shall I say one prayer in Spanish?"

Johnny said, "I guess God understands Spanish as well as anything."

José spoke the prayer, put his hat back on, and blew his nose.

"Eh, it is lucky they did not catch us making a tight group like that, those bushwhackers. That would have been a fine thing for them, all of us, in one volley, at prayer."

They went on, the herd parting around the heap of slab rock that covered Reavley's grave. The valley turned and turned again, ever narrowing. At night they pocketed the herd and gathered a lean-faced, silent group, around a tiny cook fire between the almost perpendicular walls of a side gully. The coffee was hot and weak. They gnawed jerked beef that was tough as the sole of a moccasin, and finished off with exactly three prunes apiece.

"Last of the jerky, last of the prunes," Pancake growled. "We'll have doughgod tomorrow. I don't know what in hell we'll do after that."

"Plenty of beef," Bill said in his treble. "And you won't be able to tell it from jerky, either, if we run 'em much farther. I hope those Deadwood miners haven't got their mouths set for a rare tender steak. They'll need teeth like a winter wolf to chaw *these* critters."

Johnny laughed for the first time since they'd buried Reavley. "Talk like that is poor for the cattle business. For my money, beef at its best should have some substance to it. I wouldn't want that grain-fed beef like you eat in the Union Pacific restarawnts. Now, these critters of ours are what's called in the trade 'grassers.' There's twice the strength in a pound of this beef that you'll find in that Ioway stuff. It's sort of preserved on the hoof. Cut it across the grain for eating, or lengthwise and you could halfsole your boots with it. Anyhow, old Sittin' Bull has had those miners eating pack rat and squaw root for so long they'll sit down to our steaks and think they're in Delmonico's back in Noo Yawk."

Geppert said, "If we get 'em there."

"We will."

There was no alarm during the night, none the next day. José, scouting for trail, rode far ahead and returned

190

at sundown with word that they would soon reach some elevated parklands, and after a few miles of those, could cross a rocky escarpment and drop down on the head-waters of the Spearfish. This in turn would take them north to the Redwater, and following that south again, they would reach Deadwood.

Johnny asked, "How long will it take us?"

"To the Spearfish? I theenk two days. Maybe we run these cow like hell, we make it tomorrow."

"Then let's run 'em like hell."

Johnny, Carson, and Big Bill took the early watch. They came down the canyon side about midnight, and Geppert, José, and Jardine took over. Old Pancake, who was stove up from rheumatism, cared for the remuda.

It seemed to Johnny he'd barely crawled in his blankets when he awoke with the raw feel of smoke in his throat.

The stars were hazy. As he stood, he heard a man crash down through the brush. "Fire!" It was José. "Forest fire. She's ahead, running thees way. Where the hell? I can see notheeng! Where are you?"

Instantly the camp was up. Horses for morning were already on picket ropes, saddled.

"Somebody help me with the grub," Pancake said.

Geppert and Jardine followed José into camp.

Johnny said, "We better get the hobbles off the remuda. If that herd starts to move, they'll tromp 'em to mincemeat. Better yet, everybody get an extra horse. Cut the rest loose." He rode through the dark, among jostling men and horses, calling one after another of them by name to make sure that all were accounted for.

The herd was up, bawling, milling around. The stars, visible only a minute before, were now covered by blowing layers of smoke. It made a dense, thick darkness. A man could scarcely see the ears of the horse he was riding.

Geppert said, "I got my horse fixed to lead — what in hell are we waiting for?"

Most of the others were talking, too. Johnny shouted over the voices, "Hold on and listen. Listen to what I say, otherwise we'll get separated in this smoke, and never get together. We'll head downvalley. Stop at the forks. If the herd runs, we'll try to mill 'em there. That's the big forks, about four miles. These fires run in streaks. If it goes down the main channel, we'll turn back along that branch running southeast."

They started out, leaving the herd behind. It was too dark to see and they trusted the instincts of their horses. Smoke, ever more dense, made a man's eyes water, his lungs raw. A horse stumbled and fell. José was cursing in Spanish, English, and Cherokee.

Johnny turned back. "You all right, Josie?"

"My horse! A rock jumped up and hit his knee."

"Can he travel?"

"Perhaps. It wounds me to ride a crippled horse."

"Come along. We can't let the boys get out of hearing."

Johnny waited fifteen seconds that seemed like a minute while José groped around in the dark. Behind them he could see the fire, a brownish-red line, through blanketing smoke. It ran before the wind, was carried by heat draft into the harrow V of the canyon.

"Come on, Josie. What in hell are you doing?"

"A new horse. Now we can ride."

They found their way down a bank, splashed through the creek. Johnny removed his kerchief, dipped it, squeezed it out, and breathed through it.

"Where are you?" José was now in the lead.

"Coming."

They rode at a steady trot and gallop, taking their chances among rocks, windfalls, and prospect holes.

The wind seemed stronger now. It blew smoke in dense layers with once in a while a current of clear air that was as refreshing as spring water on the desert.

The canyon turned, and turned again. They crashed deep in brush, and for a moment Johnny had no idea where they were.

"There they are now," he heard Big Bill say in the thick gloom. "That you, Johnny?"

He answered and rode, bent low over his horse, clawing brush out of his way. They descended steeply and climbed steeply. It was a dry feeder stream.

Underfoot was grassy earth. The canyon walls seemed to be nowhere close. He was baffled, turned around. Even the breeze seemed to have changed. He called to Bill, got an answer, and rode up to him.

Now he could see a little. "Everybody here?"

"All but Josie."

"I am here, bareback, leading a lame horse. Where are *you?* Where are all of us? My eyes feel like there is red pepper in them. I can see nothing."

"This is the canyon forks."

Now that they'd stopped, Johnny could hear bawling as the herd moved up. It relieved him. Often cattle will merely stand while fire sweeps over them.

Wolf Carson said, "There won't be much left to deliver in Deadwood after they run through *this* hell hole."

"They're not running. Not yet."

The canyon would contain them; rough ground would keep some of the animals moving against the current. You need plenty of room for a real stampede.

"Think we can turn 'em here?" Geppert asked.

"We might if the smoke cleared a little. I'd hate to work cattle blind as I am now."

They rode slowly across the bottoms. A cross current of wind flowed down the gulch from the southeast, carrying smoke away. Here there was only a thin fog. They could see a rocky horizon on the south; down-canyon, the smoke lay in drifts against the north wall and veiled some narrows where rock walls closed in.

Jardine said, "There's a spot to stop 'em. A man could just about block this canyon if he had an ax and could drop a couple of those big bull pines. What I wish we had is that big roan lead steer of Haltman's. They'd follow him through the dark like old Wolf Carson would follow a squaw."

The narrows were less than fifty yards off. Jardine, who was in the lead, suddenly wheeled his horse and shouted, "Ride! Ambush!"

Gunfire spurted from two directions as if it had been released by the impact of his words. Jardine was hit. Bullet shock cut the sound in his throat.

The slug knocked him off his horse. Johnny, close to him, turned his horse sharply, bent over, got him by one arm, boosted him, grabbed the collar of his shirt.

Jardine, while tall and slim, was a heavy man. Johnny fought to get his weight in balance while the horse pivoted and threatened to go sunfishing and throw them both.

They were caught in a cross fire. Bullets tore past on both sides. The horse reared, coming down with a quarter turn. Jardine, recovering from bullet shock, clung desperately. He was being dragged, his feet on the ground. Then he got hold of the saddle horn, and with Johnny's help pulled himself over the pommel.

It all had happened in four or five seconds.

The interval seemed timeless, something plucked out of space, an instant when a thousand thoughts exploded through a man's brain. Johnny had expected to be hit. Then, when the first hail of lead didn't touch him, he had the opposite feeling — he was charmed against ten thousand bullets.

He rode at a gallop, carrying with him a memory of their voices — Mixler's voice, Ellis Haltman's voice. He hadn't expected any of the Haltmans to take part in a bushwhack. But Ellis was a hothead . . .

The steep northern side of the canyon stopped them. They found a trail, started to climb.

José, in the black haze somewhere, called his name.

"Get going!" Johnny shouted back.

He didn't say any more. Didn't want to reveal his position. He had to get Jardine off somewhere and take care of his wound.

He kept riding. He still had the spare horse on a lead string. Jardine tried to pull himself upright, but Johnny said, "Stay down. Don't move any more than you have to."

The canyonside rose in a series of pitches. They were checked by talus rock. After some groping he found another trail. The smoke was very thick. It hid the sky, the ground beneath, everything. He'd have lost all sense of direction, except that the canyonside was always there, giving him his objective, up, up, until somewhere he could find safety for the wounded man.

Minutes had passed and Jardine hadn't made a sound. He was alive, though. Johnny Colt could feel the tension in his body as he fought to endure the pain.

Johnny stopped the horse and said, "Can you ride?"

Grunting from the effort, Jardine answered, "I think so. I'd be better off. This is hell. We still got the extra bronc?"

Johnny dismounted and got Jardine in the saddle. "How is it?"

"I'm all right. I can hold on."

"Where are you hit?"

"I dunno. High someplace. It hurts here, then the whole side of me feels dead."

He tied Jardine's boots to the stirrups, which he snubbed tight, and hooked his cartridge belt around the horn. Then, riding bareback on the spare horse, he led the way, hunting a steep trail, climbing, always climbing.

"Where we going?" Jardine asked.

196

"Yonder. Out of the reach of this fire. You find springs here and there along the sand-rock outcroppings. I'll fix you a spot at one of them."

"How about the herd? How about the other boys?"

"I'll go back."

"Damn it, I'm able to take care of myself from here. You don't need to —"

"Don't talk. Just hang on. If things start going black, tell me."

The movement of the horse would keep Jardine's wound open, and that would be bad. He wanted to have a look at it, but it was impossible to do anything for him in the dark. Perhaps, farther up, the smoke would thin out.

About ten minutes had passed. For a time there had been no shooting. It broke out again, and was followed by more minutes of quiet. Sometimes, when the trail was padded by evergreen needles, he could hear the bawling of cattle. A stone clattered, telling him that someone was following.

He thought with no good reason that it was José, and called, "Hey, Josie!"

After hesitation an answer came from no more than a hundred yards off. "Yes, Johnny!"

It wasn't José. It was someone trying to imitate him. He thought of Kiowa. Yes, that's who it was — that sneaking half-breed Kiowa.

Kiowa wouldn't be alone. Others, probably most of the others, would be with him.

It was too dark to see Jardine. "How are you?"

"Bleeding. One side of me's all gummy. We got to stop. I can't get my feet out of the stirrups."

"Take it easy. They're tied down. Just sit there." He dismounted. The steepness of the canyonside surprised him. It dropped off beneath his boots and almost sent him sprawling. He walked around the horses. Jardine, apparently desperate at his inability to get his boots free, was lashing around, cursing in a whisper.

"Stop it," Johnny said. "Fred, it's all right. I'll get you loose."

His voice finally registered. That, or Jardine had momentarily passed out. He got the leather untied. Jardine had slumped far over the horse's neck. He half fell, and Johnny, holding him in his arms, got him to a smooth spot on the ground.

He cut the man's shirt off. He needed light to do any more. Half expecting a bullet from below, he scratched a match. The bullet didn't come. While the match burned down in his fingers he raked twigs and pine needles together, lighted the little heap, and by its uncertain light had a look at the wound.

He'd been hit just under the collarbone. The bullet had been turned by his shoulder blade and come out the back. Both sides were bleeding, but not too badly. He made packs of wadded, blood-soaked cloth, and bandaged it as best he could.

As he worked he could hear the clatter of horses climbing the rocky trail. They kept getting louder.

He tramped out the fire and said, "Fred, can you hear me?"

Jardine moved, opened his eyes, and said, "Yeah. Sure, Johnny. Where are we now?"

"Why, I guess we're just about on the Dakota border."

Jardine had enough left in him to laugh.

Johnny asked, "How you feel?"

"I feel good. I just want to stay here. Just want to sleep."

"Pretty soon. We'll go on a piece, and you can sleep. You got to stand up now, Fred."

"Hey?"

"I say you got to stand up."

With Johnny's help he got to his feet, back in the saddle, belt tied to the horn and boots to the stirrups.

Johnny paused to listen. They were close now.

The sounds stopped. It was very still. They were listening and he was listening. He decided to wait, guess their direction, and take the opposite one.

He noticed how he was sweating. His hat was slick and thick on his forehead. He took the hat off and felt the cool passage of air. The wind was swinging a little. Soon it might clear the smoke. He wasn't sure now that he wanted it to clear. The smoke was a shield as well as a mask.

Jardine called in a voice startled and loud, "Johnny! Where are you!"

"Quiet!"

It was too late. They'd heard him. He cursed under his breath.

"What's wrong?"

"Nothing. It's all right. We better get moving."

Jardine got out a wheezing laugh. "And here I was worried about Sioux!"

"Keep right on worrying. With our luck they're probably waiting on top."

Slowly, as they rode, he became able to see things. He first thought the smoke was thinning. It was still as raw as ever in his throat, in his eyes. It was coming dawn.

Jardine seemed to be asleep. He was bent forward, left hand holding the horn of his saddle, right pressed against his chest. He rocked gently with the movement of his horse. His face looked hollow and dead.

He roused and met Johnny's eyes. "Seems like we been riding forever."

"I know. We been at it a little more'n an hour. This is pretty steep. How you feel?"

"Better, I guess. I'm just so damned thirsty."

"We'll find a spring."

The day before he'd crossed many moss-filled depressions where water appeared briefly at the surface before flowing away under the slide rock.

They kept going. They were over the canyon wall, on the bulge of the mountain, and it was not quite so steep. He found a gully and followed it. It had the damp smell of water. He dismounted and dug with his boots through moss. The moss at the bottom was barely damp. He kept climbing, leading the horses. Finally the moss felt cold through the sides of his boots, and he dug again. There it was so damp you could squeeze water out of it like a sponge. He cleaned his hands, worked until he'd caught a pint in his hat. He carried it to Jardine and watched him drink.

"How was it?"

"Good!" Jardine panted for breath. "My God, it was good!"

"Sure. That ain't ordinary water. That's got strength in it, like green turtle soup."

It was quite light now. He could see around him, through smoke, for upwards of fifty yards. Timber grew sparsely in clumps, and there was a chance that a high wind might shift around and blow the fire to them, but that was a chance he'd have to take. It was as good a spot as he could hope for.

He made a bed for Jardine among fallen trees, rebandaged him, washed his face and chest with wet moss.

"How you feel now?"

"Good. This is the best bed I had since Texas."

"Wound hurt?"

"No. Nothing hurts. I feel like I was in a feather bed. I just want to lie here. Just sleep."

"All right. I'll leave a hatful of water. Listen now." The man had closed his eyes and Johnny had to grab his shoulder to awaken him. "Listen. They're still after us. Don't say anything. No matter what, don't say anything. Just lie here. They can't see you. A man could walk right yonder to the bank and not see you."

He watched Jardine's eyes, wondering if there were any understanding in him.

"I'm leaving a hatful of water right here. Give me your hand. And here's your six-shooter. Right there.

I'm going now. I'll keep those bushwhackers following me. I'll lead 'em away yonder. And I'll double back. Listen to me. I don't know how long I'll be, but I'll be back."

CHAPTER
SIXTEEN

Johnny Colt climbed up from the little gully. He stood, resting his elbows on the saddle, letting fatigue run out of his body. Above and below lay the mountainside. Blending with the gray curtain, it seemed endless. The density of the smoke kept changing. There were times when things a few dozen yards off would look milky and uncertain, then an eddy of wind would bring a long vista into sight.

He waited, wondering if he'd lost pursuit. The answer came in movement and blue gun shine. That breed! He could smell trail like a wolf. He moved instinctively, drawing the Winchester from its scabbard. A bullet stirred rocks with a hard rattle near his feet, explosion closely following.

His horse, lunging with his head up, almost broke away. Holding tight, with the bridle twisted around his left wrist, he let the animal drag him. He dug his boot heels and brought it to a stop.

His gun was ready but he didn't fire. Drifting smoke closed in. A second bullet buzzed the air past his cheek. The report was from farther off, from up the canyon. They'd split up to climb the mountainside, and now they were converging on him.

"Johnny!" the wounded man called.

"Damn it, I'm all right. I told you to keep quiet. I'm pulling out now, maybe until after dark. I'll take them with me. Don't worry, I'll be back."

Riding one horse, leading the other, he went on. After sixty or seventy yards he stopped, not because the horse was tired but because he didn't want them to lose sight of him. He wanted to lead them a long way from Jardine's hiding place before losing them.

Each time the smoke blew away they'd start shooting, trying for a lucky hit. He didn't answer them. He didn't have cartridges to gamble. Only the full magazine and eleven in the loops of his belt. Plenty of .45's, but not enough .44's. You always ran low on the ones you needed.

After half an hour he reached the crest.

The mountain was actually a long ridge broken by little knoblike summits. A cliff, about a hundred feet high, dropped off ahead of him. A long slope lay below the cliff, then forest and more cliff and talus rock. The smoke was thinner on that side, and dimly he could make out the bottom with here and there the flat shine of water.

Wind had almost cleared the summit of smoke, making the air good to breathe. He headed eastward and reached a spot where the cliff had been cut by a landslide.

They saw him and started whanging away. A sliver of rock stung his cheek. They were closing in from three directions, obviously believing that the cliff would stop him. The landslide channel was his only chance. He

204

dismounted and started down, sliding across dirt and bare rock.

The horses tried to balk. With a heavy hand on the bridle he brought them along. His high heels and spurs were a help, breaking his speed. An unforeseen danger were the trampling hoofs. He avoided them, ended against slab rock at the foot of the slide.

He had to straighten the saddle, then he mounted and followed a goat trail that doubled back along the base of the cliff.

It was narrow, pressed by the cliff on one side, hemmed in by huge, blocky rock slabs on the other. The horses had no choice except to go straight on, so he let go of the reins, and with the rifle in his hands kept watch of the cliff rim above.

A horseman appeared suddenly. The man carried his rifle across the pommel, and it was already pointed slightly down. Johnny Colt had no time to aim. He merely brought the Winchester around, caught its stock in the bend of his right arm, cocked it, and pulled the trigger.

The bullet flew a trifle to the right. The horse reared. On sloping rock, his legs went from under him. The rider fired wildly. He dropped his rifle and made a grab for leather.

The horse dumped him, lunged, trampled over him, galloped out of sight.

The man, on his stomach, slipped across the edge of the precipice. He slipped slowly, boots first, fingers clawing the smooth rock. He screamed from terror, and for the first time Johnny realized who it was. The half-breed, Kiowa Jim.

Kiowa hung for a second, caught by a rock projection. Then he fell with a shower of stones chasing him. He struck on his back with his arms wide. His broken body was wedged between rocks only an arm's reach from the trail.

The horses were frightened of him and refused to pass. Cursing, Johnny cut the extra horse free of the lead string. He felt for his neckerchief to fashion a blindfold. It wasn't around his neck. He remembered wetting it the night before. It was a damp ball in his hip pocket.

Finally he got his mount past. Other men were now atop the cliff. He could see the shadows of their movements, but they didn't show themselves. They didn't want to follow Kiowa over the edge.

For eighty or ninety steps he was hidden by the slightly overhanging face of the cliff. Then some pillars of rock gave protection. The trail narrowed. There was a second cliff with the trail slanting down it. It was so narrow the horse's side threatened to push them into the abyss. He dismounted and walked with one hand against the rock wall, the other holding the bridle. He set his mind not to think where a misstep would plummet him.

He'd been hidden for an eighth of a mile. Now the trail placed him in view. No rock underfoot here. He walked on yellowish clay, among dwarf juniper. A bullet from long range stirred a geyser of dirt. He kept going, on and on, a twisting, often slow descent.

He mounted and rode through pine. Now, in the bottoms, he could see the twin marks of a road or a travois trail, some placer pits, the roof of a rude lean-to shanty.

Minutes had passed since the last shot. He kept looking back. No one was following. That wasn't right. It gave him a sinking sensation to think that they might have turned back and discovered Jardine.

Then he saw three horsemen to his right nearing the bottoms. They'd taken a shorter route and were closing in.

It was a temptation to get down with his rifle and say, "Come and get me." He couldn't. He had to get back to Jardine.

Making a quick decision, he turned sharply and spurred at a gallop, trying to outrun them up the side of the valley, through timber.

From above he'd been unable to appraise the rough topography. Now he saw that his course was suicidal. It would lead him to a steep switchback, and the switchback to the bottom directly into their guns.

He slowed his horse. There was the roof of that shanty again. Closer, near the foot of the slope, was a big, rusty heap of dirt. It was a hard-rock prospecting dump, and its size told him that a tunnel of considerable depth must have been driven into the mountainside.

Any deep tunnel necessitated an air shaft. If the tunnel went straight in the mountain, the air shaft, driven vertically, would be nearby. He reined in, stood in the stirrups, and looked for it.

It was no more than eighty feet away, a mere collar of logs rising a couple of feet above the ground. It almost escaped detection. There was no dump of waste rock such as marked the tunnel. It had been driven upward from below.

He dismounted, crouched, looked into its black depths. He dropped a pebble, heard it rattle and rattle before clicking to rest in the bottom. A steady upcast of air told him it still communicated with the tunnel. There was no ladder, but pole cribbing and cross-pieces had been set to hold the walls, and he'd be able to climb from one to the other.

Working swiftly, he dragged deadwood branches to conceal it. Then he remounted and rode at a gallop down the last switchbacks to the valley bottom.

A rifle bullet whipped past with a sting of closeness. He saw men and fired back as rapidly as he could lever his Winchester. His bullets drove them to cover. They were beyond the cabin, content to keep him cornered until help arrived.

He found cover close against the hillside. The mine dump, a flat projection terminating in a pole tipple, gave more concealment. The horse balked at the tunnel entrance. He blindfolded him, led him inside.

There, in the cool dampness, he sat down with his rifle across his knees, knowing he'd be able to kill every gunman Mixler had if they came for him. Which they wouldn't. He laughed. No, you're damn right they wouldn't!

CHAPTER
SEVENTEEN

He was tired. His legs felt paralyzed. He dozed between waking and sleeping, and a sound brought him up, alert.

Someone had spoken. For an instant he imagined the voice came from the mine depths behind him. Then he realized it was only echo.

"Johnny, I know you're in there!" It was Mixler.

He didn't answer. He rolled a cigarette and dry-smoked it. A stone rattled near the portal. Then Mixler again, closer now.

"Johnny, can you hear me?"

The voice kept ringing for a long time in the dark rock walls of the tunnel. It reminded him of José's guitar, when, lying close to it in the still prairie night, one could hear the tiny ringing sound that always hung to the strings. The mine was like that, if one listened closely enough.

A gunshot deafened him. He had to stand to restrain the horse. Someone had fired upward, into the portal. A sulphurous smell drifted toward him.

Mixler shouted, "You want to get out of there alive? Then come out with your hands up!"

Alive! His lips twisted in a smile. They'd kill him the second he showed himself.

He waited, and after a long time he heard a thud and smelled drifting dust as they rolled boulders from above, gradually cutting off the light, closing the portal.

It became quite dark. The horse, after some momentary nervousness, stood quietly. Johnny tied him to a timber and groped his way down the tunnel.

It was not a crosscut tunnel, driven straight to intercept a vein. It followed the vein and was unpredictably zigzag. Finally he saw light, very dim, from above. The air shaft.

The shaft was also crooked, driven for the twin' purposes of ventilation and exploration.

He left his rifle and climbed up the timbers. It was a small shaft, a scant four by four. He was able to rest with his legs braced wide. At last he saw the sky, broken into little irregular patches by the brush he'd thrown over the shaft collar.

Twenty feet from the surface he stopped, braced his legs, breathed, listened. There was no sound. He tried to guess at the time. At least half an hour had passed since the portal was closed.

It was not difficult to work his way to the surface through dead branches. Sunlight, coming through smoke and spruce trees, seemed very bright.

He crept downhill, hidden by timber. Hunkered, with a view of the valley, he kept watch while several minutes passed. Satisfied they were all gone, he found a wooden bar and levered away the big, rocks that blocked the tunnel. His horse was waiting. There was no room to turn him in the narrow confines — his toughest job was getting him backed out.

By noon he was with Jardine, who had just awakened and was looking for another drink of water.

"How is it now?"

"I'm all right. I feel like I could stand up."

"Don't push yourself too hard. Don't move that side if you can help it. I'll get you a drink, then we'll have to go down and find the camp — if there is one."

All was quiet where the ambush had met them with flame and bullets the night before. The fire had run in long, black fingers across the ridge to the south. They moved among scattered cattle, downstream, and came across Big Bill, José, and Wolf Carson around a tiny campfire, washing trout on willow sticks.

Big Bill almost shed tears of relief at seeing him, but José only said, "Ha! What did I tell you? He was born to die in a legal manner with the rope of the law around his neck. Johnny, did you hear about my guitar? Broken, smashed under the hoofs of those Texas cattle. Oh, my poor guitar, my sweetheart, you are gone and now how will I serenade the women of Deadwood?"

Big Bill said, "Keep still and help me with Jardine. Can't you see he's taken a slug in the shoulder? Easy now. Easy."

They got him comfortable on some spruce boughs. Geppert and Pancake weren't around. Johnny asked about them. No one had seen them since the night before. He ate, then he got up and swapped saddles to one of the fresh horses.

José was watching his face. He knew Johnny perhaps better than any other man alive, and the expression he read there made him stand and hitch his gun belt.

"You go for a ride?"

"I guess."

"You maybe have an idea of visiting Mixler?"

"Let's us visit him before he visits us."

"He's not through with us?"

"Mix won't be through with us till we're dead. He thinks I'm dead already. Now he'll come back for you — and the cattle."

"So?"

"So let's look for him. I've run from him more'n any man alive — or dead. I had reason to do it, but I haven't any longer. He don't need to look for me now."

José laughed with a flash of white teeth. "Now, thees is the way Johnny Colt should talk. Thees is the Johnny Colt I loved to ride with. Now is the time we go looking for him." He looked at Bill. "Are you coming?"

"You're damned right I'm coming!"

They left Wolf Carson to take care of Jardine, and rode at a stiff pace down canyon. It was late afternoon and growing cool.

José said, "Perhaps we ride in the wrong direction. Perhaps that big lobo and his killer wolves are already tracking down Al Geppert and poor old Pancake with his rheumatism."

"I doubt it. They had even less sleep than us. They'll camp someplace. The cattle are scattered. They think they got plenty of time."

212

At twilight they crossed a saddle in the ridge. Johnny pulled up and pointed with an outflung arm. "I reckon that's where they plugged me in the mine, only yonder, farther up. Good water in this valley. They'd be fools not to light here and rest."

"Ha! Fools if they did!"

Later, a pin point glimmer of fire came through the deep shadow that filled the valley. José laughed and said, "You are a fine man with a hunch, Johnny. Why with these good hunches are you such an easy mark for every sharper at three-card monte?"

They rode downward along a crooked gulch, around pine-covered hills. Only Big Bill seemed cautious. Johnny Colt was slouched in the saddle, hat over his eyes, apparently half asleep. José sang softly, in a scarcely audible voice, the words of some border song.

"Damn it, keep still!" Bill whispered.

José laughed. His laugh was like quiet music. "Bill, it makes you nervous, the thought that soon I will outdraw Señor Shoots-in-the-Back Glynn?"

"There'll be guns besides his."

"So perhaps you would like to make a wager. One thousand dollars, Señor, that at the pay-off it will be José on his feet and Star Glynn on the ground when —"

"Who'll pay me if you lose?"

"Wait! Johnny Colt, to you I will confer the great honor! If I should die, which any gypsy will tell you is impossible, to you I will bequeath the leetle black book containing a record of my debts right down to the last centavo."

"That damned book!"

"You curse it when you are rich in its pages already?" José got the book out and looked at the first page, squinting to read the figures by twilight. "You say I am a man who forgets his debts? Look, in pesos the first entries! Here the sum of one thousand, seex hundred and seventy-five pesos to Señor Manuel Guzman, who would have been my father-in-law, but alas, it was not to be. She broke my heart, that girl, so I was sad and could not eat for two weeks, but lived on wine. And this next —"

Bill asked, "Where do you get to that ninety bucks you laid me for that first night I run into you down in Guadalupe?"

"Ha, that! It is here someplace. Away over here in the middle of the book. I had traveled far before meeting you, and I had borrowed here and there — a leetle bit. You know, in the evening like this, with danger all around, I am sometimes struck by an awful fear for these debts. What if some of these men I borrowed from are dead? Johnny, if I should die and you were to ride back, paying my debts along the way, I would have you do something nice for these dead men's families."

"Yeah," said Johnny Colt. "I'll try to remember that."

It had been thirty minutes since they'd seen the fire. Now, in the deepening gulch bottom, it was quite dark. The odor of burning wood came to them on the breeze, and somewhere in the chokecherry bramble a horse snorted.

Johnny said, "This is it!"

"You figure to ride right up?" Bill asked.

214

"Well, maybe I will. Yes, I'll ride up. You boys get on each side." He jerked his head, indicating opposite sides of the gulch. "Stay back a little. Might be a sentry out. I doubt it. Mixler will feel pretty safe, but there might be. If there is, he'll stop me, and I'll let him know you've got him covered."

He rode alone the last two hundred yards. Light of the fire was always visible, but broken into irregular patterns by intervening brush. Men were seated around it. He couldn't tell how many.

One of them stood, bent over, moved away. It might have been Billy Six-Spot.

The path he followed, skirting the brush, was almost free of stones. His horse made no sound as he advanced. He'd lost track of José and Big Bill. No sentry stepped out to meet him. Horses, hobbled and grazing in the bottoms, had their heads up, but his approach didn't make them run.

He pulled in, sat in thoughtful contemplation of the fire for a long thirty seconds. Without looking, he knew that José had come around on the other side of the brush. He heard the slight clink of a spur as his heel came in contact with the ground.

He dismounted, tied his horse, and walked through brush, following a narrow little trail, holding twigs away.

He stopped at the edge of firelight. Men were sitting and lying on the ground. Across the fire, staring at him, lay Andy Rasmussen.

Andy had seen him. His eyes were fixed. His jaw had sagged. He didn't seem to be breathing. He'd been eating a broiled grouse, holding it by the drumsticks, tearing flesh off with his teeth. In amazement he'd lowered the bird until it rested in the dirt.

Johnny grinned at him. It wasn't a pleasant grin. He disliked Rasmussen, had contempt for him, and the smile showed it.

He counted five others by the fire. Besides Rasmussen, there were Star Glynn, Evas Williams, Ellis Haltman, a cowboy called Alky, and Mixler. He wondered about Billy Six-Spot. Maybe Billy had been killed.

Mixler was sitting cross-legged, his back turned. The long trail from Texas had taken him down, removed the last ounce of fat from him, dehydrated him, and yet he was big. Big, and lean, and rangy like an elk that had come through a hard winter.

Mixler was talking. Something about the herd. As Johnny listened, the words came to him. ". . . No, when that fire runs out they'll drift back with the grass and water. We'll hold the main bunch on the Belle Fourche and send back for 'em. A few days' graze won't hurt. We'll be across the Yellowstone before September first."

Evas Williams, noticing the fixed nature of Rasmussen's gaze, turned and saw Johnny Colt.

He started as though to lunge to his feet, and stopped himself on one knee. It was almost reflex to reach for his gun, but he didn't.

"Sure, Evas, live for a while," Johnny said, and stepped into the firelight.

Men sprang to their feet, but nobody went for his gun. Mixler was up. Huge and erect, he took a backward step. For just a second his face was slack with surprise, as though he were staring at a ghost.

Johnny said, "Funny thing about miners. They generally dig two holes, just like a prairie dog."

Mixler recovered himself. He pulled his lips back, showing his powerful teeth in something that resembled a smile. "Well, I'll be damned! You know, Johnny, a man's got to admire your kind of guts. I'm going to kill you, but I still got to admire you."

"Might not take so much guts. I might have you outnumbered. That's something you have to gamble on." As he talked, his eyes were on Mixler, but he kept watch of the others, too and when Glynn, looking very slack and casual, started to drop back, he said, "Now, Star, that might be a number-one way of committing suicide. How you know but what I got six men out in the bushes? Why, six men would take care of everyone here."

Rasmussen, watching him, spoke from the side of his mouth in a whisper scarcely audible. "He was alone up the canyon. He was holed up alone. One down, rest of 'em scattered. He's bluffing."

"If you believe that, try going for your gun."

Rasmussen wouldn't do it. Mixler, perhaps, or Glynn, or Evas, but not Rasmussen.

Johnny said, "I came for you, Mixler. Before heading over the ridge for Deadwood, I came for you."

Mixler's eyes kept moving around, probing the shadows. He licked his lips. He jerked his shoulders back with a laugh. "But you got an ace in the hole!"

"Nobody's going to kill you but me. I got a proposition for you. You leave your men by the fire. We'll walk over yonder, across the creek. There's not much light, but there's enough. We'll settle it there, the two of us. I fought your kind of fight one night, now you fight mine. But maybe you haven't got that kind of guts."

Mixler twisted his lips down. He hated Johnny, he'd hated him from the first night when he'd noticed Lita Haltman watching him.

"Why, you cheap gun hawk!" Mixler spat. He stood with his hands on his hips. "I'll fight you with guns or I'll fight you with my hands. And when I'm through, you won't go over the ridge to Deadwood. You won't go anywhere. To hell with crossing the creek. You're not ten seconds away from being a dead man!"

Mixler's massive shoulders sloped forward a trifle. His eyes were very intent. Beyond him, Star Glynn was on one knee, staring beyond them into the dark.

Neither José nor Big Bill was in that direction. The warning hit him like the buzz of a rattler. It was Billy Six-Spot. He'd been standing guard somewhere, and now he was coming up from the shadow.

Johnny started to turn. It was a casual movement, but it ended in a dive to the ground.

He struck on an outflung hand. Guns exploded. Two guns — one so close on the other that their sounds came in a single clap.

A bullet hit him. It was like being slugged by a hammer. It made his ears ring. It took away his sense of

218

direction. His body seemed to float. The scene veered and slid across his eyeballs.

He'd never lost sight of Mixler. He saw Mixler draw. He saw, and could do nothing about it. It was a nightmare thing with his mind working, but his body frozen, apparently able to make no move.

Mixler had turned the gun on him. Flame and explosion burst in his face. He could feel the whip and burn of powder.

He was no longer on his side, on the ground. He was on one knee. He'd hit the ground rolling, and the bullet had missed him while he was rolling. He'd never actually been still. His brain had been racing ahead of his body.

His own gun was in his hand. He had no memory of drawing it. It was merely there. It seemed to draw and aim and fire by itself. He was dully conscious of the hard buck of it.

There was shooting all around him, the darkness laced by gunfire, the night rocked by gunfire, but to him there were only the two of them, himself and Mixler.

Mixler was hit. He was knocked back half a step. He grabbed at his chest, but the six-shooter was still in his hand. He still faced Johnny Colt.

He shouted — a curse, a challenge. The words were unintelligible. They were a roar from his throat. He came forward, gun clutched in his big hand, firing with each step. Johnny hit him with another bullet, but it didn't drop him. He didn't hestitate. He was like a rampaging bull buffalo, willing to be killed if he could also kill. Mixler took another bullet. He fired again. It tore the ground between Johnny's knees. His steps were Gargantuan. He stumbled, went to his knees. His eyes stared. He got up, took two more steps, cocked and pulled the trigger. The hammer only clicked. He stopped and swayed. His eyes on Johnny still held a glint of understanding. He knew at that final instant that Johnny was alive and he was dead. Still, there was no surrender in him. He tried to lift the gun, to use it like a club, but the effort failed midway, tension left his muscles, went face down, head bent under him, forehead digging a furrow in the soft clay earth.

Johnny stared at him. He looked around. He was still trying to recover from bullet shock. He saw Star Glynn on his back with arms wide, one hand almost in the fire. There was shooting in the outer darkness. He started to walk, but from behind a hand grabbed him. He turned and saw José.

"Away from the fire. There might still be bushwhack bullet."

"Where's Bill?"

"Sending them on their way. You hear the Winchester. Ha! There is a man with a Winchester, Big Bill. How do you feel?"

"Like somebody hit me with a hammer."

"It was that bushwhacker, Billy Seex-Spot. I saw the shine of his gun just as he lifted it, but alas, I did not have time quite to save you. See? Your sleeve is heavy with blood. You took a bullet in your left arm."

"What the hell happened? That's Star Glynn, isn't it?"

220

"Sure. Did I not say it would be heem? Did I not say I would pay heem for the bushwack of Reavley? But he had more guts than I thought. We shot it out across this fire. Now be still and I will bandage the wound."

"I'm all right. We better get hold of Bill." He called, "Bill!"

Bill's voice came from the uphill shadow. "Here! You better stomp that fire out or they'll circle and make wolf bait of you."

José laughed with a bright flash of his teeth. He had his shirt off, tearing it in strips for bandages. "No. They will have little fight left. What was it the poet said? 'When the head is chopped off, the bird theenk only of flapping his wings.' So with those gunmen, I theenk they will fly far and stop only to fight when another has dollars to pay them."

Geppert and Pancake had returned to the camp on Ironrod when they got back. Two days were spent hunting cattle, and with most of the herd they pushed over a high backbone of the country toward Spearfish.

It was evening, and Johnny, riding the drag, reined to roll himself a cigarette.

He looked back and to the north. There were foothills, prairie, the purplish breaks of the Belle Fourche, and more prairie. Still farther over the uncertain, grayish horizon lay the Yellowstone, and after the Yellowstone, the vast, almost untouched plains of Montana, the land where grass grew to a tall steer's belly.

221

José saw him and came back at a gallop. "Johnny! Why do you stop? We must hurry. Just over the hill, maybe only tomorrow away, are there not the lights and women? Is there not music and good red wine? Is there not the Deadwood of our dreams?" He closed his eyes, entranced, and strummed a dream guitar, singing:

> "Ay, ay, ay, ay!
> Canta y no llores . . ."

"Sure, Josie. I'm sure with you for that Deadwood."

He was thinking that he'd spend a week in Deadwood. No more. Josie would be broke by that time. Broke and borrowing money. In three weeks he'd have all of them broke, including Tom Mace. He'd leave after a week, while they still had something left. With fresh horses, they could head back up the Belle Fourche, cross the Little Missouri, and meet the herd. Later he would find McCrae and Jason to pay them off. But first, the herd.

It would be tough on the Haltmans, taking that big herd through shorthanded. He had nothing against the Haltmans. Ellis was a hothead, but lots of men are hotheads at the age of twenty-one. Vern and Tommy were all right. And Lita . . .

Sometimes, at the most unexpected moment, the memory of Lita would hit him, and she'd be there again, beside him, slim and eager, her hands on his shirt, her dark eyes looking up at him. Yes, he'd find Lita at the Yellowstone, too.